He's ba-ack!

Amy stared with shock into Tom Nicholas's dark glare and thought that if any one thing could have made this day worse than it already was, it was this. Him.

Had one of her glamorous sisters met an old lover, she thought wryly, it would have been in a moonlit garden or by the glow of a dying fire. But she had to be caught in the corner of a soggy bathroom, in torn blue jeans, trying to retrieve a blanket one of her two-year-old charges had exuberantly flushed down the toilet. Typical.

Still, she was up to the challenge. Tom Nicholas couldn't get to her anymore. She was committed to being a new and better Amy. She folded her arms and drew a breath for calm.

"Hello, Tom," she said coolly, lifting her hand to sweep the hair out of her eyes. "What are you doing here?"

In her mind she heard him reply, "I've come for you, Amy. I'm sorry I left. I've been in agony every day since. I've thought about you. Longed for you, desired you, missed you with absolute desperation. Say you forgive me. Please."

In reality he said, "I'm here about your ad."

Dear Reader,

We're delighted to bring you a very special sequel to Muriel Jensen's wildly popular "Mommy & Me" trilogy. Like us, you fell in love with the three babies who were born on the same day in the same hospital to three single moms. Not to mention falling in love with the three very sexy heroes who became their daddies!

Now those three cuddly newborns have grown up into a trio of mischievous toddlers with toothy grins and gleaming eyes. And they've got their matchmaking antennae out for their day-care provider, Amy, and her lost love, Tom.

Just wait to see what Malia, Chelsea and Garrett are up to now!

Happy reading!

Debra Matteucci
Senior Editor & Editorial Coordinator
Harlequin Books
300 East 42nd Street
New York, NY 10017

Muriel Jensen
KIDS & CO.

Harlequin Books

TORONTO • NEW YORK • LONDON
AMSTERDAM • PARIS • SYDNEY • HAMBURG
STOCKHOLM • ATHENS • TOKYO • MILAN
MADRID • WARSAW • BUDAPEST • AUCKLAND

For Jessica, Amy, Jacob, Ja'Lissa,
Chevana, Kanisha, Andrew and Julia

ISBN 0-373-16688-5

KIDS & CO.

Copyright © 1997 by Muriel Jensen.

This edition published by arrangement with Harlequin Books S.A.

® and TM are trademarks of the publisher. Trademarks indicated with ® are registered in the United States Patent and Trademark Office, the Canadian Trade Marks Office and in other countries.

Printed in U.S.A.

Chapter One

MALIA: Well, here we are—doing time again. I told you flushing Chelsea's blankie wasn't a good idea. Now she's stroking out and we're in the slammer till our moms get here. Good going, Foster.

GARRETT: Relax. Amy will call a plumber, Chelsea'll get her blankie back, and we'll get to go outside 'cause Amy'll think we need to work off steam.

MALIA: You're such a bozo. It's raining. We never go outside when it's raining.

GARRETT: Well, I'd had about all I could take of that animal-sounds book. I thought a little action would perk up the afternoon till the big kids get here. I like that Truman dude. He can spit Cheerios all the way to the fireplace!

MALIA: I know. That's cool, but he's always getting time-outs in the big chair. Here comes Kate with Chelsea. Tell her you're sorry. Give her your bear.

GARRETT: No way.

MALIA: Okay, but she's gonna scream till it's bye-bye.

GARRETT: Geez. Women! It was just a dweebie blanket, Chelsea. You got to get rid of the thing before you go to school, anyway. Here, you want my bear? Kate? Kate! Take me out, ple-e-e-ease! I don't care if it's raining, I want to go out on the slide. How about the sandbox? I won't put sand in the air conditioner this time, I promise. Kate? Chelsea, what are you doing with my bear? Ow!

CHELSEA: Take that, you macho piglet! That was my blanket. My mom says I can carry it around until I'm forty if I want to and this is what I think of your bear!

MALIA: Not on his head, Chels. It's his weak spot. Come on, you two. Amy's trying to run a respectable day care here. How will it look if some mom comes by to look it over and you're duking it out in the playpen? Hey, look. The bus is here! It's the big kids!

"AMY! THE BUS IS HERE," Kate Murray called out. "But don't worry. I'll get them their snacks, and I'll put on *Babe* for the babies!"

Amy Brown, armed with a plunger and a wire coat hanger she'd pulled apart to serve as a probing tool, sat on her knees in front of the toilet. She was surrounded by wet towels she'd put down to sop up the water. She groaned at her assistant's announcement.

Great. Now Truman, the crime boss, Darcy, the investments queen, and Rodney, who owed the cuss box $112.75, had arrived to round out the lineup of felons at Kids & Co.

"Thank you!" Amy shouted back, not because she

was grateful for the news, but because setting an example with the "magic" words had become a habit for her after six months as a family day-care provider.

She forced the extended coat hanger down the toilet, hoping against hope that the blanket hadn't gone very far, that she wouldn't have to hire a backhoe and dig up the yard to find it—as she had to do three weeks ago when Garrett flushed a twelve-inch stuffed Keiko the Whale to freedom.

The coat hanger refused to go any farther and she drew it back, praying there would be a ten-inch square rag of blanket attached. There wasn't.

From the living room she could hear Chelsea Jeffries screaming over her loss.

"No, no, Chelsea!" Kate was saying to the accompaniment of the sound of something that squeaked hitting something that screamed. "Beating Garrett with his bear, while very satisfying personally, will not bring your blanket back. Here. Give me the bear. Ouch! Chelsea!"

Above that was the sound of two eight-year-olds and a nine-year-old running to the kitchen. She could hear the sounds of the refrigerator door being opened and closed and cupboard doors slamming while Kate was probably preoccupied with the screaming toddlers.

Amy closed the lid on the john, propped her elbows on it and dropped her head in her hands. She didn't know whether to laugh at Kate's textbook-psychology-catchphrase approach to child care, or cry over the chaos that she knew reigned in her living room.

It was a good thing the parents of the toddlers were all friends of hers from her days as promotion and public relations director at Riverview Hospital. Otherwise any stranger walking into this facility this afternoon would probably have her license pulled.

The older children hadn't fit in elsewhere, so she was in no serious danger of losing them, but that was not necessarily a comfort at the moment.

She had two other children enrolled who were blessedly normal—Pete and Eddy Nicholas, nine and twelve, Malia Nicholas's brothers, but they came only two afternoons a week when there was no football practice after school.

But she was getting inquiries all the time, and she needed more space if she was to provide the kind of day care she really wanted to offer. Remodeling the barn behind the house had seemed like the ideal solution.

The building had been wired and plumbed by the previous owner, but it needed many inside amenities before it could be inhabited by children. And she had visions of cupboard and closet space, a second kitchen, a roomy bathroom.

The playground equipment between the house and the barn was perfectly placed for the summer, but in Heron Point, Oregon, it began raining in late September and didn't stop until May. She imagined converting one half of the barn into a kind of indoor playground.

But that would only happen if she could find a builder she could afford. So far the bids were outrageous, and if she had to keep hiring backhoes and plumbers because of The Mad Flusher, her dreams of expansion would be pushed farther and farther out of reach.

Her family might help her if she asked, but she'd come to Heron Point and taken the job her uncle had found for her at the hospital to escape the look of disappointment in her parents' faces.

Her father had inherited a textile factory from his father, and though, as far as Amy recollected, he'd never contributed much to running or improving it, he'd had a competent staff, and so the company had been a success and their family comfortable.

Her mother, a society maven and a beautiful woman, had groomed her three daughters to marry up, as though their home on Long Island was some country place in Regency England.

Jane, Amy's older sister, was beautiful, petite and brilliant, and had claimed the attention of the scion of a wealthy Boston family in her second year at Yale.

Peggy, Amy's younger sister, was beautiful and very tall, and had caught the eye of a photographer at a Junior League charity function. Before she knew it, she was working as a professional model.

The last Amy heard in a birthday card from her mother in April, Peggy was working in Paris through the summer.

Amy had been her mother's only failure. She had no interest in her looks, in social contacts, or in the young men who ignored her for those very reasons. She was happy enough with her degree in education and a position in a school library, but her mother kept shaking her head over her and murmuring "poor Amy."

So she'd come to Heron Point to take control of her life. But the illusion of starting over had lasted only long enough for her to launch the Model Mommy campaign for the hospital's birthing rooms opening, fall in love, then have love walk out on her as though she'd been just any old affaire.

So she'd decided to do something for herself—not to meet the family's expectations of her, and not to comply with some societal rule that expected her to find a man whose idea of a wife was a tall, slightly gawky blonde who really wanted to belong but couldn't quite make it happen.

She'd left the hospital and with a small inheritance from her uncle put a down payment on this big old house at the edge of Ethan's Woods. She had to make this work. She would not fail.

She didn't want to hear another "poor Amy."

She groaned and lifted the lid on the john, feeding the hanger slowly down, knowing the future wasn't going to brighten for her until she had the present in order.

"Right," she thought as the sound of dishware crashing to the floor came from the kitchen. "Like that's going to happen."

TOM NICHOLAS HEARD the persistent doorbell and tried to make his way toward it. But with a blinding headache and the remnants of sleep clouding his brain, he wasn't doing very well. He bounced off of the back of a chair, crashed into the coffee table and limped toward the annoyingly cheerful sound while his shin throbbed painfully.

Before he could reach the door, he heard a key turn in the lock and the door flew open, launching two figures into the room. He squinted against the glare to identify them. Oh, God. Just what he didn't need. His brother and his best friend.

He put one hand over his eyes and held the other hand out, hoping to stop them from moving farther into the room. "I know, I know. I should have told you I was back. But I got in late last night and..."

"Oh, shut up." Jave, his brother, walked right past Tom's halting hand and into the kitchen. "I wasn't expecting to hear from you," he called over his shoulder.

"You've been wandering the countryside for almost two years with nothing but a card or a call every couple of months to let us know you're alive, and Mom and Nancy and the kids worried about you. Why would I expect to be informed that you've moved back into town? I'm the one remaining person in your circle of family and friends who's still talking to you, but, hey… Haven't you even made coffee yet? It's almost three o'clock.''

Nate Foster, Tom's friend, looked him up and down and fell into the chair that faced the television. "A word of advice,'' he said. "If you're going to try to sneak into town, you should park your truck in the garage instead of the driveway. Nice one, incidentally. You must have made big bucks with Healey Construction.''

Tom sank into a corner of the sofa, resigned to accepting Jave and Nate's loving but brutal concern. But he was not in an accepting mood. He'd been awakened this morning shortly before eight by the sounds of the sanitation truck, and he'd gone to the window and looked out on residential Heron Point and wondered what in the hell he was doing here.

He'd just finished working on a hotel in Tucson four days ago when he'd looked around at the hot, dry landscape and had the very same thought. *What in the hell am I doing here?* With sweat pouring down him and nothing but mesquite and tumbleweed for miles, he'd longed for the four-mile-wide river, for the evergreens, the coastal breeze, the moist and fragrant air that made even the deepest summer day feel like he was rafting on a lake. For Heron Point.

He'd been so homesick for Oregon that he'd quit Healey on the spot, turned down a considerable raise and a plea to stay with the crew as it moved south to Tempe, packed his truck and headed north.

It had been long enough, he told himself. He'd put the specters of his past behind him before he'd even left Heron Point, but he'd still had to get away to learn to live without them. Guilt had governed him for so long, it had pushed him from the fire-fighting career he'd loved, driven him into an aimless isolation that had kept his entire loving family frantic with worry. Just before he left, Nate, who had been treating a homeless woman, proved to him that he hadn't been hearing things the night he and Davey stormed into the burning hotel, that a woman *had* been screaming, even though he hadn't been able to find her. At the time, he'd felt as if he'd sacrificed Davey for a woman who didn't exist. Davey had died while waiting for him.

No one had understood his need to get away. They'd insisted the issue was resolved. He wasn't to blame for anything. Why did he have to go away now?

It had been hard to explain that guilt had become his identity, and that without it, he had to rediscover himself. His mother had told him he'd always overanalyzed everything. Nate told him he was nuts. Jave told him he was running away.

Amy had closed her door in his face. So much for the love and devotion she'd pledged just two nights earlier.

Angry and confused, he'd left town and kept just a minimum of contact, knowing if he was ever going to find himself again, he had to do it without the family and friends who were always so quick to support and defend him.

He'd had to learn to depend upon himself again, to

learn that he was worthy of his own trust, that he was whole once more.

He'd thought he had, until he'd looked out the window that morning and felt the impact of all that was familiar in his hometown It was one thing to feel heroic in foreign surroundings, but quite another to come back and face the demons that had wrestled you down.

"You look like you ought to start a grunge band," Jave said, two steaming mugs hooked in the fingers of one hand, one in the other. He was wearing a suit. He and Nate, Tom guessed, must have just left the hospital.

"How'd you do that so fast?" Tom asked, sniffing suspiciously at the light brew in the cup.

"It's a powdered instant Jo ordered for Mom," Jave replied, sitting on the other end of the sofa. "I made it in the microwave."

Jo Jeffries owned Coffee Country downtown, a coffee bar patronized by everyone in Heron Point.

Tom took a careful sip and found that it was sweet and tasted of almond. He held back a grimace. Construction site coffee often doubled as mortar, but he'd grown used to it.

This stuff tasted like melted candy, but at least it was hot.

"You heard from Mom?" he asked, trying to sustain the mood of civility as long as possible. "She wrote me that you and Nancy and the kids gave her a trip to Europe for her birthday."

Jave leaned an elbow on the back of the sofa and turned sideways to look at him. "Yeah. She's with a tour in Scotland. She's having a great time. She's not due home until Thanksgiving." He looked around at the bag Tom had propped against the coffee table, the tool boxes he'd brought in to clean up, the jacket over the back of a dining room chair, the sandwich plate and empty potato chip bag from the meal he'd made himself when he'd arrived last night. "That'll give us time to bulldoze this place and start over."

Tom drank more coffee, tuning out the sweetness and concentrating on the heat and the caffeine. "Don't nag, all right? I just got here. I'll get organized."

Jave ignored his reassurances. "How are you?" he asked, and waited for an answer with that analytical, older-brother concentration that had always annoyed Tom yet somehow sustained him.

"I'm fine," he said, almost surprised that in some deep-down, elemental way he really was. All he had to do was figure out what to do about his life now that he was.

"You look like the last stages of swamp fever," Nate observed.

Tom ran his hand over several days' growth of beard on his chin and through hair that hadn't been cut in seven weeks, and laughed. "Yeah, well, I'm not a doctor, so I don't have to look like a George Clooney wanna-be like you guys."

"You don't even look as good as the Unabomber."

Tom laughed again. "I know. But the last few days on the job were a real squeeze, then it was a three-day drive home, so don't hassle me. I'll clean up, then you'll be sorry because Karma will be wondering why she married you instead of me."

Nate shook his head slowly. "You *are* in the last stages of swamp fever."

"So, you want to come over for dinner," Jave asked, "and join Nate and Ryan and me for handball tonight?"

That sounded like a lot of effort at the moment, but he was looking forward to seeing Nancy and the kids.

And a homecooked meal—even Nancy's cooking— would be a nice change from the last three days of fast food on the road.

"Yeah. Thanks." He pointed to the suitcase propped against the coffee table. "Somewhere in there I've got some things for the kids."

Nate frowned. "Nothing for us?"

"I've brought you my sublime skill," Tom said grandly. "I'm sure you must have some project on the old A-frame that needs remodeling or repair. How's the deck holding up?"

"Great," Nate replied. "We spent a lot of time out there. You know..." He dug into the pocket of his jacket with a casualness that was almost theatrical.

Tom knew immediately that something was up. Jave took a magazine from the coffee table and perused it, as though detaching himself from what was about to unfold.

They'd used this trick on him before. They plotted something together, purportedly for his own good, then one or the other of them presented it in a way that would not suggest collusion. It was a device they'd employed many times when he'd been trying to put his life back together after the fire.

He waited while Nate made a production of exploring his pockets. Jave appeared to be completely absorbed in *Needlework Quarterly*.

"Ah, here it is!" Nate handed him a newspaper clipping. "If you're back in business in Heron Point, you'll need work. I just happened to notice this when I was having lunch."

"I thought you just noticed my car on your way home?"

"No. Karma noticed your truck when she drove past

to go to the Scupper. She called the hospital to ask me if I knew you were back.''

Tom blinked. ''Karma…was going to the Scupper Tavern?''

Nate rolled his eyes. ''She does their books, amoeba brain. Read the ad.''

It was a small ad from the classifieds. Accepting Bids On Barn Remodel. Call Kids & Co. Day Care.

Tom looked up. The ad seemed simply to be a good lead on a job. He'd made and saved a lot of money during his two years in Arizona, but he'd stashed it in savings to build his own place one day, and he was eager to get back to the variety of work offered in general carpentry.

And work done at a day care would mean a lot of parents would see it, and that could mean more work.

Had he misjudged his brother and his friend?

He doubted it. Nate was drinking his coffee with studied calm, and Jave appeared to be memorizing a knitting pattern.

''I suppose the day-care provider is a gorgeous single woman,'' Tom guessed, pocketing the ad.

Nate and Jave exchanged a look. ''As it happens, she is,'' Nate replied. ''This could get your business and your social life off to a good start.''

''You two are so transparent. Just because you were involved in a wedding frenzy and a baby boom two years ago, don't think you're getting me involved.''

Nate gave him an affronted look. ''Did anybody say anything about weddings and babies?''

''Not me,'' Jave replied from behind the magazine.

Tom snatched it from him and slapped it on the table. Then he caught Jave's arm and pulled him to his feet.

With his other hand, he caught Nate and dragged him along as he headed for the door.

He backed them up to it and caught each collar in a fist.

"Now, you two listen to me," he said with quiet sincerity. "I'm back in town less than twenty-four hours and you're already working my life like a piece in a chess game. I do not belong to you!" His voice rose despite his efforts to remain calm. He swallowed and began again. "I am no longer your burned-out little brother—" he focused on Jave, then turned to Nate "—or your needy friend. I've got it together, and I'm back. I want to be a part of your lives, but don't try to find me women or create work for me or otherwise manage my life, or you'll need an orthopedist! Do I make myself clear?"

"Very."

"Sure."

"Good." Tom pulled them away from the door, pushed them aside, then opened it. He smiled amiably at his brother. "Then I'll see you at dinner, and you—" he slapped Nate's shoulder "—at the gym."

"So you don't want help of any kind," Jave said, stopping at the porch stairs, "but you don't mind being fed."

"Food is always above the rules. Pleasure to see you both."

Tom closed the door, then peered through the small square of window in the top to make sure they left.

They walked side by side down the steps, two men in dapper suits who looked like an ad for Armani. When they reached the bottom of the steps they turned to each other, exchanged a high five, then laughed as they walked to Nate's car.

Tom didn't like the looks of that at all.

Just to prove to himself that he was impervious to their machinations, he called the number in the ad.

A young woman's voice answered. Children's raucous voices and crying babies were audible in the background.

"This is Tom Nicholas Carpentry and Construction," he said. "I'd like to make an appointment to see the barn you'd like remodeled and offer a bid."

"Oh. Hold on, please."

He waited. She was back in a moment. "Come by anytime," she said. "The barn is in the back. You have the address?"

"Yes, thank you. I'll be there in half an hour."

Tom showered and shaved and wished fervently that he'd done laundry. He went to the closet in his room and found a pair of casual beige slacks he hadn't bothered to pack when he'd left two years ago. He pulled them on and found them snug. He'd acquired glutes in the intervening time.

In the bottom drawer of his dresser was a long-sleeved green knit sweater he'd never liked because it made him look like a dandy. He pulled it on, thinking that if he was going to wander around a day-care facility, he'd better look as little like a reprobate as possible.

Tom rapped on the front door of a big, turn-of-the-century farmhouse about a quarter of a mile from Nate's place at the edge of Ethan's Woods, and introduced himself to an attractive but very serious-looking young woman. He told her he was going back to the barn.

Behind her he could see an empty playpen, a little girl sitting in a big chair watching television, and two boys on the carpet, playing with cars and trucks.

"That's fine," she said with a stiff smile.

Jave and Nate had really lost it, he thought as he made his way across a neatly trimmed back lawn to a red barn the same vintage as the house. The young woman was practically a child herself, and looked as though she wouldn't know how to laugh if she were given directions.

He pulled the barn's big double doors open and turned his attention to the project. He turned on a light switch on the wall, and could see the plumbing and wiring had been brought in, and that there was a deep laundry tub on the far side.

Cheap paneling had warped on the walls, and the floor squeaked. The windows were rotten, and a flimsy partition apparently intended to separate the large space into two rooms was falling down.

The structure, however, looked sound. He climbed up into the loft to check the beams and found them dry and free of rot. The floor of the loft was sound and would allow that space to be made into an interesting room or office, depending on what the owner wanted to do with it.

He climbed down again, pulled a small piece of paneling away and found that the walls, too, were dry. The leaking window frames had probably been responsible for the condition of the paneling.

He sat on a rough wooden bench and made a few calculations. He put together a bid in three parts. The first, a deluxe remodel, included a dropped ceiling, a stairway to the loft on a second floor, a new floor downstairs, new windows and a wall dividing the space into two rooms.

A moderate job included all the features of the deluxe job, except for the dropped ceiling.

If the client was operating on a really small budget,

he could do just windows and floor and whatever cosmetic work was preferred.

He copied the figures legibly onto a piece of letterhead on his clipboard and headed back to the house.

He was intercepted halfway across the lawn by one of the boys he'd seen in the house. He was towheaded, freckled and scrawny in the way of little boys whose metabolism outdistanced even their great consumption of food.

And this one seemed to be made of sheer energy. He sprang along beside him as though his shocks were bad.

"Hi! Are you gonna fix the barn?"

"Maybe," Tom replied. "I'm going to bid on the job."

"We're gonna play in there in the winter. You're the fourth bidder. The other three were too high."

That was good. He'd put together a conservative bid, hoping it would help reestablish him in Heron Point. After that, the quality of his work would build his reputation. When he'd left the fire department and gone into business for himself four years ago, he'd had more work than he could handle within three months.

"I'm Truman," the boy said, still hopping along beside him.

Tom detoured to go around to the front of the house. "Weren't you president once?" he teased.

The boy punched him in the arm. "Everybody tries that joke. That was Harry Truman. I'm Truman Fuller."

Tom stopped at the bottom of the porch steps to offer his hand. "Hi, Truman. I'm Tom Nicholas."

The boy had a good grip—dirty, but good. "I've got friends named Nicholas. Pete and Eddy. And Malia. She's a girl, though, and a baby."

"I'm their uncle." Tom walked up the steps and Truman followed.

"Cool! The hero from the fire?"

Tom felt the beginnings of the old familiar wrenching in his gut. But he could stop it now. He bore no guilt for it. That was over. Resolved. This was now.

"Not a hero," he corrected the boy gently, rapping on the door. "I went to try to save somebody, but she was already gone."

"But if she'd been there youda saved her!"

The boy's eagerness to invest him with heroic qualities touched him.

The door was opened by the grave young woman. She invited him into a large living room. There were toys everywhere, an empty playpen, and rocking horses on springs, rockers and wheels. The girl still occupied the chair, but the other boy was now stretched on his stomach on the sofa, engrossed in the television.

Something apparently happened in the action that the boy didn't like and he said emphatically, "S---!"

"Rodney!" the young woman said. "You owe the cuss box another quarter. And I'll have to tell your father you're slipping again."

"Well the Gargoyles just got attacked!"

"'Darn it' would have been just as effective a response. I understand your need to express distress, but you're in the presence of a lady."

Rodney frowned. "Where?"

The girl, clutching a fairly large box that seemed to be wrapped in plastic, replied, "Me, stupid," without even looking away from the television.

The woman put a hand to her forehead and closed her eyes.

"I can just leave this with you," Tom said quickly,

afraid the woman was about to have a breakdown. "If you're interested, we can talk about it when it's convenient for you."

"Oh." She shook her head. "I'm not the director. She does want to talk to you. She's in the bathroom. We're having a plumbing crisis."

"Garrett Foster flushed Chelsea Jeffries's blankie down the john!" Truman seemed to find it exciting.

Tom grinned. "No kidding." When he'd left Heron Point, his niece, Malia, and Garrett and Chelsea had been a little over three months old. Now they were two years old.

It had been a curious twist of fate that the babies had all been born at Riverview Hospital on the same day, and that their parents had become the best of friends thanks in part to Amy Brown.

First he'd felt lucky to be part of their warm and riotous group. Then, after the holidays, when they'd all settled into their contented routines, he'd been unable to find his own contentment. So he'd left.

But he was back. And getting work was going to be an important part of his readjustment process. So he put the past out of his mind and followed the young woman across the living room and down a corridor that deposited them in the partially open doorway of a bathroom, with Truman still at his heels.

The woman knocked twice on the door, announced, "He's here!" then turned Truman bodily around and led him away with her.

"Hello?" Tom pushed the door open the rest of the way.

The sight that greeted him drew a quick smile and a gusty sigh of masculine appreciation from him.

A woman was bent over the john with a plunger, her shapely derriere in jeans swaying with her efforts.

"Just a...minute," she said, yanking hard with the plunger. She planted both feet more firmly, affording him an even more delectable view.

Then the little rug under her left foot slipped, the plunger went flying, and she fell backward with a little scream of alarm and a wild flailing of arms.

Tom caught her without even having to move. He extended both arms and she fell into them, hers clutching at his as her head and shoulders crashed into his chest, slapping silky silver blond hair against his mouth and chin.

With his arms full of her, he was overpowered suddenly by several alarming familiarities. The shapely tush, the scent of jasmine, the soft breast around which his right hand was shaped—and the fact that he was here at Nate's and Jave's suggestion.

He put the woman on her feet none too gently, spun her around—and found himself looking into Amy Brown's startled gray eyes.

Chapter Two

Amy stared with shock into Tom Nicholas's dark glare and thought that if any one thing could have made this day worse than it already was it was this. Him.

But for an instant she saw the anger shift in his eyes, letting something else take its place. Something gentle and quiet that allowed her to let all the hurt and anger go and remember what it had been like to love him for two months.

Actually, he hadn't loved her all that time; theirs had been a very volatile relationship. She'd come to Heron Point trying to find self-confidence, self-esteem. And then she met Tom, who was at a point in his recovery from the fire when he blamed himself for his friend's death and tried to refuse himself all happiness.

But she'd pushed, and he'd weakened, and for a few blissful weeks she'd been happier than she'd ever been in her life. Then they'd made love for the first time, she'd touched his burned leg when he'd asked her not to, and the encounter had ended in disaster.

Shortly after, Nate had discovered that there had been a woman in the old hotel the night of the fire; that Tom hadn't heard phantom screams. They'd been real—very real.

And just when Amy had expected that Tom, free of the self-inflicted guilt, might turn to her again, he'd come to her apartment to tell her he had to leave—and he didn't know for how long.

She didn't think she'd ever forget the pain of that moment, how it had felt to see him standing there, thinking he'd come to tell her he loved her, only to discover he was leaving.

She'd screamed at him that she was tired of waiting for him to stop running away from happiness and that it was over. Then she closed the door—on him and on all she'd hoped to have with him.

And here he was, one glimpse of his dark brown eyes decimating the control she'd finally acquired over the loneliness, destroying the confidence she'd built in herself one careful step at a time. It had been such a long way back. And that was reason enough to let her anger reignite.

She yanked out of his grip and took a step away, the narrow confines of the room relegating her to the corner between the john and the tub.

Had one of her glamorous sisters met an old lover, she thought wryly, it would have been in a moonlit garden or by the glow of a dying fire. But she had to be caught in the corner of a soggy bathroom.

Still, she was committed to being a new and better Amy. She folded her arms and drew a breath for calm.

"Hello, Tom," she said coolly, lifting her hand to sweep the hair out of her eyes. "What are you doing here?"

In her mind she heard him reply, "I've come for you, Amy. I'm sorry I left. I've been in agony every day since. I've thought about you, longed for you, desired you, missed you with absolute desperation. Say you forgive me. Please.''

In reality, he said, "I'm here about your ad." He reached to the floor for a clipboard he'd apparently dropped when he'd caught her. He turned it over to reveal a sodden newspaper clipping. The sheet of paper under it, however, was covered with figures and considerably dryer. "I've given you three options. If any of them appeals to you, call me."

He removed the sheet of paper with the figures, handed it to her and turned to leave.

She should have just let him go, but this was the new Amy—no longer afraid to speak her mind. "I can't believe you had the nerve to come here," she said, balling the sheet of paper in her hands. "And *three* options?" She widened her eyes in theatrical surprise. "I thought you were a take-it-or-leave-it kind of guy."

He turned in the doorway, his formidable chest rising and falling as he drew a breath—for patience, she guessed. She was pleased that she'd annoyed him. She remembered that he'd hated having to talk about what he felt.

"I came here," he said with exaggerated calmness, "because I didn't know Kids & Co. was *your* place. Otherwise I'd have known there was nothing for me here. And if we're questioning motives, why did you *let* me come? I called for an appointment first."

"The message I got was that Somebody or other Carpentry and Construction was coming by to bid on the barn," she said, her hand tightening around the ball of paper in it. "It never occurred to me it could be you. And you're right. There is nothing for you here. You killed it."

He leaned a shoulder in the doorway with an arrogance she hadn't seen in him two years ago. "*I* killed it?" he asked. "Who slammed the door in whose face?"

"Who ran away?" she snapped back.

"I...left," he said quietly, "to try to figure out who I was, with the thought that that would be better for you as well as for me. But you're the one who closed the door in my face when I tried to explain that. So, metaphorically, I'd say you're the one who ran."

She made a scornful sound and tossed the paper wad in the air. "Yeah, well, you've always had a myopic view of the world. Thank you for coming. Don't call us, we'll call you. We've had several other bids. Would you let me pass, please?"

She tossed the paper wad again and he caught it as it came down. He remained where he was, filling the doorway. "Three bids, I understand," he said. "And all of them too high."

She looked a little disturbed that he knew that. He enjoyed it. "Well. I'd have done a good job for you, but never mind. We'll just consider the bid withdrawn."

She was quiet for a moment, and he thought he saw an instant's flash of regret in her eyes. Then she met his with a haughty glare. "I think that would be best. Goodbye, Tom."

He backed out of her way into the hall and let her pass before him, leaving the bid in his haste, feeling a desperate need to get out of this house and into his truck. She always had the ability to take a simple situation and confuse him about which way it should go. He hated that.

She was the one who hadn't understood. *She* was the one who'd closed the door on him after he'd shared his deepest concerns. Why should *he* feel guilty because for an instant her gray eyes looked hurt and anguished?

She marched past him into the living room.

"Did he get the job?" Truman bounced around her the way he'd bounced around Tom. "I vote for him. He's Pete and Eddy's uncle!"

Amy put an arm around Truman's shoulders, encouraging him to be still. "I know who he is, Truman. But he's not really…what we need."

She went to open the door for Tom, the last three words spoken with subtle significance.

Tom started through the door, headed for his truck and his new life in Heron Point without the irritations this woman had applied to his old one.

Then he stopped. It occurred to him that the door closed in his face had burned in his gut for two long years. During that time he'd accepted that it had been his fault that that had been the final word. He should have banged on the door until she opened it again and told her what he thought of her capacity for understanding. But he'd had his pride.

Well, he still had it, but she wasn't going to close the door on him again.

"You're wrong there, Amaryllis Brown," he said, leaning aggressively over her. "I think I have precisely what you need. Truman!"

"Yeah?" The boy came to him eagerly.

"Will you hold the door open for me, please? I'll be right back."

"Sure!"

Heart thumping with leftover surprise, anger and a trace of excitement she thought of as battle fever, Amy stood in the doorway impatiently as Tom went to his truck. His words echoed in her ears—"precisely what

you need," "precisely what you need," and the, er,
battle fever rose a little higher.

He opened the back of the truck and removed a wide
loop of metal that he slung over his shoulder. A plumber's snake.

He ran lightly up the porch steps, marched past her,
then went into the bathroom, with Truman in pursuit.
The two children who had been watching television
crowded into the small space with Amy.

Tom fed the snake into the toilet, assigning Truman
to hold the remaining loop of cable while he worked.

He met an obstruction almost immediately and carefully withdrew the snake as though reeling in a trout.
The end of the cable appeared, a wad of baby blanket
attached to the end of it.

"Chelsea's blanket!" Darcy exclaimed, her cellophane-wrapped box clutched in her arms. She looked
up at Amy in wide-eyed disbelief. "He found it!"

Amy gently disentangled the dripping patch of blanket from the end of the snake and lobbed it into the
sink. A little soap and disinfectant, and Chelsea could
have it back.

"Thank you," she said stiffly, relieved that she didn't
have to call a plumber and that Chelsea would be happy
once again. But she hated that it was Tom Nicholas
who'd accomplished that. And before he could think she
considered the gesture anything but business, she asked
briskly, "What do I owe you?"

His eyes went from the snake he was recoiling to her,
their darkness filled with rebuke. "Perhaps that's a
question you should ask yourself?" he suggested.

Then he turned and left the room, the snake dangling
from his hand like a lariat. The children ran after him.

"Mr. Nicholas!" she shouted authoritatively, stopping him at the outside door. The children ran ahead of him to his truck.

"Yes, Miss Brown?" he asked politely, the formality between them edged with sarcasm.

She squared her shoulders and closed the distance between them. "I appreciate your help," she said, "but I will not let that be a favor. I want to pay you for your time."

"I'll bill you," he said, turning away.

"Tom!" she said sharply, grabbing his arm and turning him back. "I insist!"

She knew she was in trouble the instant his eyes met hers, dark and turbulent with anger. She braced herself, not sure what form it would take.

Tom looked into her stubborn frown and wanted more than anything to shake the square-shouldered resolution in her, to rattle all that unyielding determination that made her so sure of what she wanted—and made her know it wasn't him.

The children nowhere in sight, he caught the back of her neck, pulled her to him and opened his mouth over hers. In the kiss was anger for two years of loneliness, disappointment that she hadn't fallen on him with apologetic tears as he'd have liked in some old-world corner of his mind, and personal pain that she could look so good when he'd been so miserable.

Then the softness of her, the familiar scent of her that brought back other times, other kisses, the delicious, moist taste of her after two long years of eating sand gentled his anger and made him forget he was taking his payment in punishment.

He felt her lean into him and kissed her deeply, thoroughly. Then she gave him a sudden, vicious shove and he let her go.

"You egocentric Neanderthal!" she shouted at him.

"You parsimonious old maid!" he returned. "It *was* a favor. Live with it." He turned, heady with anger, and suddenly, painfully, discovered what had happened to the children.

They were bunched behind him on their hands and knees, watching something in the floorboards of the porch. He fell over Truman and saw Rodney and Darcy scatter as he began to go down.

He heard shouts, screams, then the staccato thump of his body against the steps as he hit each one on his way down. With a curious clarity in the heart of danger, he saw the terra-cotta pot on the stone walk and knew he was headed for it—quite literally.

Then he was one with a pretty bunch of purple pansies, pain exploded in his head, and the world went black.

TOM FELT AS THOUGH he were being used for croquet practice, as though someone had a foot on his face and was hitting him in the head with a mallet.

He decided against opening his eyes, knowing it would hurt.

"You're *sure* he's all right?" That was Amy's voice, high and concerned.

His heart palpitated in response to her worried tone. Or was it thumping because of his injury?

"Amy, I'm sure." Nate's voice was patient but had an air of finality about it, as though he'd answered the question before. "He's coming around. I know someone losing consciousness is scary, but it isn't as dangerous as it seems. And this guy's got a head like granite."

Tom opened his eyes at that and found that he'd been right. It *did* hurt. He was apparently on the sofa, and the lamp on the end table behind his head shone right in his eyes.

When he winced against it, a hand moved it away.

Three faces leaned over him—Nate's, Amy's and Truman's.

"Granite?" he asked Nate as he put a hand to his throbbing head. "Are you supposed…to talk about patients like that when…they're out?"

Nate pushed Tom's eyelid up and flashed a light into it. "What's wrong with granite? It makes great monuments and lasts forever. What's your name?"

"Elvis. I'm back."

"I could find a reason to inject you with a really big, dull needle. Your name?"

"Tom Nicholas, six foot two, 193 pounds, born August 25, 1963. One brother, James Victor Nicholas, who tends to enter into collusion with one Nathan Borman Foster for the purposes of playing with my life. What else do you want to know?"

Nate held three fingers up in front of Tom's face. "How many fingers?"

"Three. If there were not a woman and a child present, I would break them for you."

"Hostility is not good for your condition."

"You mean because it could affect your condition— negatively."

"Look." Nate leaned over him, his gaze level and purposeful. It was his emergency room face. Tom had seen it several times before. "You've had a nasty blow to the head. You seem all right, but you never know about these things. You need to be watched."

"I'm fine." Tom tried to sit up.

Nate helped him, then steadied him as the room spun. Tom quickly closed his eyes and tried to right the world again. He opened his eyes cautiously. The ceiling was back where it belonged.

"You need to be watched tonight," Nate said, "and your mother's away. I'm going to call Jave."

"No!" Tom said too emphatically. The sound hurt his head and set the room spinning again. He closed his eyes. "No," he repeated more quietly. "You know how he is. He'll sit over me and have his whole house in an uproar. Besides. You guys were going to the gym tonight."

"I think we can forgo that for one night."

"No. I won't go to Jave's. I'll be fine at home. Mom's got a cordless phone. If I feel ill, I'll call you."

"No way." Nate stood. Tom opened his eyes to keep track of him. "If you won't go to Jave's, I'm taking you home with me."

"No. You're as bad as he is."

"Tom. This is not a choice. If you don't cooperate, I'll call 911, have you brought in and admitted."

Tom glared at him. "You do that and I'll rivet you to your front door."

Darcy's face appeared over the back of the sofa. "When you fall on somebody's 'propity,'" she said tutorially, "you can take them to court and get lots of money. My mom works in a lawyer's office."

"Bonehead!" Rodney said. "He fell over *us*. It's our fault."

"So. It's Amy's propity. She's supposed to keep it safe. He can get lots of money."

Amy accepted this last indignity in a day that had been filled with them. "Thank you, Darcy," she said dryly, then turned to Nate with a fatalistic sigh. "Why doesn't he just stay here? I'm not going anywhere and I won't hover. I've got several extra rooms upstairs, I'll see that he has some dinner, and if he has a problem during the night, I'll be nearby.''

Nate's expression didn't change, but she thought she saw a little flare of victory behind his professional firmness. She questioned it with a raised eyebrow, but he turned to Tom, who did not look pleased with the suggestion.

"I'm going home," Tom insisted.

"You're staying here," Nate corrected him, "or you're going to the hospital. It's as simple as that."

Rodney sat companionably beside Tom. "Hell of a mess, huh?"

"Rodney, the word *hell* isn't allowed," Amy said. "You know that. Please don't say it."

"My dad says it all the time. And lots worse."

"I know, but that's the problem we're trying to solve, remember? You're both trying to learn to use real words rather than swear words. And so far, he's doing a lot better than you are." Amy smiled at Nate. "You'd better get home to Karma. Thanks for coming. I should have called 911, I guess, but I thought if you were home, you knew his case history and everything...."

"I'm glad you called me." Nate gave her a quick hug. "If there's a problem, call me no matter what time. Take it slow, Tom. It'd probably be a good idea to stay down until dinner. I'll be back in the morning before I go to the hospital."

Tom ran a hand over his face, perfectly willing, suddenly, to follow the suggestion. He felt very tired, and since everyone seemed to be squarely set to prevent him from doing what he wanted to do, retreating into sleep seemed like a good idea.

"Sure," he said, then with a grudging glance up at his friend, added, "Thanks."

"You're welcome. See you in the morning."

When Nate opened the door to leave, a burly man in grubby jeans, boots and a work shirt came into the room. Rodney left Tom's side, calling, "Hey, Dad!" He pulled the man to the sofa. "This is Tom and he just fell over me and Truman and Darcy and the doctor came and he might have a concussion!" That was all reported excitedly like a child might have announced the birth of puppies or the arrival of the ice cream truck. "He has to spend the night 'cause his mom's gone and somebody's gotta watch him!"

The man leaned over Tom and asked tentatively, "Tom Nicholas?" Then, as though a closer look had assured him that he was, he beamed a smile, extended his hand and said in a big voice, "Boomer Sorenson. You built the poolroom at the Scupper. Me and Paulie Petersen held the Sheetrock on the ceiling while you put it up."

Tom remembered the burly giants who'd offered to help when his T-brace collapsed. He tried to surface from his weirdly disconnected state and offered his hand. "Hi, Boomer. You saved my skin. How's it going?"

"Great!" He patted Rodney's shoulder proudly. "My boy, Rodney."

"Yeah. We've met."

"You going to be okay?"

"Sure. Just need to rest."

Boomer turned to Amy. "How was Roddy's language today?"

Tom watched Amy open her mouth to reply, then reconsider and smile. "He's trying hard, Mr. Sorenson, but I hope you'll keep reminding him."

Boomer nodded, looking a little sheepish. "I'll just

have to plainly do better myself. Well, let's go, son. Your mother's picking up a pizza on her way home from work. Good to see you, Nicholas. Thanks, Amy."

While Amy saw Rodney and his father to the door, Darcy returned with a pillow and a blanket. The cellophane-wrapped box still clutched in her arm, she plumped the pillow for him and urged him down to it with nurselike care. Then she covered him with the blanket.

"You want your shoes off?" Truman asked.

Before Tom could decline the offer, Truman was unlacing his steel-toed Wolverines and pulling them off—or trying to.

"Don't you guys ever go home?" Tom asked.

Darcy knelt on the floor beside the sofa as though ready to be of service. "My mom doesn't come till six. And Truman's dad is always late. Sometimes he gets to eat here. Amy makes good stuff."

Yes. He remembered that.

He tapped a finger against the box in Darcy's arm. "What's in there?" he asked.

Darcy held it toward him so that he could see it. "It's a Beautiful Bride Brenda, 1995." In its original wrapper, the box revealed, besides the smiling doll in all her wedding finery, a bridal bouquet, a garter, a suitcase—presumably for the honeymoon trip—and a casual outfit complete with brimmed hat and tennis shoes.

"Wouldn't you be able to play with it better," Tom asked, "if it was out of the box?"

She shook her head, wide green eyes solemn. "It's not to play with. Brenda is a collectible. It's an investment."

"An investment."

"From Grandma Browning. If I don't play with it,

Mom can sell it in a couple of years and make some money. My dad never paid stuff, so we have lots of dots.''

"Debts," Truman corrected her, still yanking unsuccessfully on Tom's shoe.

"Debts," she repeated. "You want a glass of water?"

"I think the best thing we can do," Amy said, returning now that the Sorensons had gone, "is let Tom get some rest. Let me help you with that, Truman."

Tom, lying on his side, watched her support his leg in her arm as she slipped the other hand inside the heel of his shoe and directed Truman to pull on it. The shoe came off.

Tom had never thought of his ankle and heel as erogenous zones, but as she grasped the other ankle under him, tugged it gently sideways to get a grip on it, then slipped her fingertips inside the heel of his shoe, he felt a jolt of electricity that might have accompanied a far more intimate touch.

His breath caught somewhere in his throat. Fortunately, he wasn't called upon to say anything. She readjusted the blanket over him, told him briskly to rest, then led the children off with her.

When Tom awoke, the room was dark and the tantalizing aroma of dinner wafted toward him. He hadn't eaten anything since the very early hours of that morning, and he reacted like Pavlov's dog.

He sniffed, trying to analyze what it was. Something traditional. Something his mother fixed. Something he hadn't had in two years.

"Pot roast and vegetables!" Truman announced.

The light behind Tom's head went on with blinding suddenness and Truman's head appeared over the back of the sofa. "I'm supposed to see if you feel like eating, or if you'd rather sleep. Amy says she can fix a plate for you that you can microwave later if you want."

She'd like that, he thought with sudden, inexplicable rancor. Well, if she could invite him to spend the night as though there'd never been anything between them, as though they'd never begun a beautiful night together that she'd ultimately ruined—then he could play the same game.

She no longer meant anything to him except a reminder that women could be good company, but a man shouldn't get serious about one.

He could be as unaffected by seeing her again as she was by seeing him.

Tom made his way to the table, Truman supporting him solicitously if unnecessarily with an arm around his waist. He and the boy sat across from each other at the table in a pretty green-and-beige dining room with an old-fashioned hutch filled with teapots.

He focused on them, spotting a small one sprigged with rosebuds that he remembered Jave and Nancy buying for her the Christmas before he left. When she'd lived in the small apartment, he'd teased her about the collection because there hadn't been enough space for her to display them together, and she'd distributed them around the house.

They'd been on the counter in the kitchen, on the coffee table in the living room, on the dresser in her bedroom.

Somehow their reunion in the antique hutch seemed to express that she'd accomplished something, that she finally had what she wanted, and he couldn't help a certain twinge at the knowledge that she'd done it without him.

Of course, he reminded himself, if a woman was willing to head off on her own without a second thought to the man in her life, then it would be easy for her to make strides.

It was the caring that held one back, the attention given to someone else's needs that took focus and energy away from one's own goals.

Well. He wasn't going to make that mistake twice.

Tom glanced at the clock. It was six-forty-five. Darcy had apparently been picked up, but Truman still waited. He wondered what kind of life the poor kid had with parents who didn't bother to come for him until it was time to put him to bed.

Amy appeared suddenly with a polite smile and a platter of succulent-looking beef and aromatic vegetables. She disappeared again and returned with a basket of rolls and butter.

"Coffee?" she asked Tom.

He smiled with the same removed courtesy. "Please. No cream, no sugar."

"Straight," she said. "Yes, I know." She gave him a quick, judicious glance and she was gone again.

He fought annoyance and concentrated on the wonderful food. In deference to her hospitality, though Nate had forced her to offer it, he was determined to spend the night in her home without a confrontation. Even though every glance she sent in his direction seemed to berate or condemn him. Responding would only mean it mattered to him, and it didn't.

Over dinner, she asked politely about his two years in Arizona, and he explained about the chain of hotels he'd helped put up in five different cities.

"Did you get to Tombstone?" Truman asked.

Tom shook his head. "No. We were in the northern half of the state. Phoenix, Flagstaff, Kingman."

"Did you see any cowboys?"

"Yeah, a few. They use helicopters now, you know."

Truman frowned. "I wish I could time-travel, you know? Like in *Bill and Ted's Excellent Adventure*. Then I'd meet famous marshals and great Indian chiefs."

Tom was a little surprised by his interest in the past. "What about astronauts and basketballs stars? They're right here, today."

"But history's alive with great people."

That seemed like an unlikely observation for a fidgety, physical child, and Tom teased him with a grin. "Really. Where'd you hear that?"

"My mom," Truman replied. "She taught American history. She liked the frontier part best 'cause her great-grandma left Missouri on a wagon train and ended up in Tombstone. Her husband was a marshal for a while."

"No kidding?" Tom regretted his disbelief and turned the grin to a smile of interest. "What happened?"

"She died."

"Your mom's great-grandma."

"Yeah. And my mom. She had cancer."

Tom guessed by the look in the boy's eyes that it hadn't been that long ago. It wasn't extreme pain as much as the simple disbelief that someone he'd apparently considered indestructible could have died.

"Me and Dad moved here from Portland to kinda start over."

"Yeah," Tom said, relating to the need to start fresh, though it didn't seem fair that a little boy should have to. He should be able to remain connected to what was familiar. "Well, this is a good place to do it. Heron Point's a great place to live."

Truman gave a noncommittal shrug. "I like Amy, but school's not so hot. They yell at you for *every*thing."

"Truman's dad is the new principal at the high school," Amy said, reaching for the boy's empty milk glass and pushing away from the table. "He has a lot of beginning-of-the-year work to do, and he's putting in some extra time learning about the school. So Truman's spending a lot of time with me."

Truman smiled at Amy with unabashed heroine-worship. "I like that part."

Tom bit back a smile and turned to Amy with mild reproof in his eyes. "Another conquest," he observed as Truman helped himself to more beef.

"One of my wiser ones," she said sweetly, managing to convey the message that Tom was in another category altogether.

Chapter Three

Tom didn't like Steve Fuller's looks. Oh, he was pleasant enough, shook his hand when they were introduced, behaved in a concerned and apologetic manner when Truman explained excitedly about the fall, even offered to pay for the medical expenses incurred.

But it was all a play for Amy, Tom knew.

She seemed to be gushing. She explained about calling Nate, that he was Tom's friend, and that there probably wouldn't be any expenses. Then she thanked him softly for asking.

Her voice always softened when she was attracted. He remembered. It had happened with him.

And now this tall guy in a suit with a body that said he thought for a living instead of wielding a hammer was bringing her voice down to a throaty murmur.

She helped Truman into a light fleece jacket, then walked him and his father to the door.

Tom pretended to be interested in the paper. Amy and Fuller were lost in their own quiet laughter as they discussed something he couldn't hear, and they didn't notice him watching them over the top of it.

Then Amy leaned down to hug Truman, Fuller put his hand on Amy's upper arm in a gesture that wasn't precisely a rub but was obviously intended to express affection, and Amy walked them out onto the porch.

Tom leaned sideways to try to see what happened next, but they were out of sight.

Then Amy was back and Tom straightened, frowning in concentration over what he pretended to read.

"Got a girlfriend?" Amy asked as she gathered up a cup and plate off the end table. "Or do you just like to look at the pictures?"

Tom lowered the paper in confusion. "What?"

She pointed the cup at the section of newspaper he held. "You've been studying that Magic Moon Lingerie insert for ten minutes." Then she went to the dining room, took a simple green teapot from the hutch and disappeared into the kitchen.

He slapped the paper down and got up and followed, pausing after three quick steps to regain his equilibrium. Rapid movement made his head thump.

Steady once again, he went through the dining room and into the kitchen. It was like walking into a bower— a bower where midgets lived.

The room was green and white, the walls covered with ivy-patterned wallpaper. A large table was tucked into a nook, and a dozen mismatched chairs painted green surrounded it.

"I was trying to remain available," he said with strained dignity, "on the chance that you needed help. I've seen suits operate before."

She put the teapot on the counter and the cup and plate in the sink. Then she filled a teakettle with water. "Suits," she repeated, going to the stove. "You think men in suits operate any differently than men in tool belts?"

He leaned against the counter as she reached into an overhead cupboard for two cups and a flowered tin.

"No," he replied, "but a woman sees a guy in a tool belt, she knows she's dealing with trouble. A guy in a suit creates the impression of being harmlessly cerebral, then you drop your guard and he's got you right where you might not want to be."

She smiled at him over her shoulder as she opened a drawer and retrieved a tea strainer. "What makes you think I might not want to be there?"

"Past experience," he replied. "You're afraid of a relationship, remember?"

He thought he saw the jab register in her eyes, but she turned them to the task of spooning tea from the tin into the strainer, so he couldn't be sure.

"I think the blow to your head," she said as she placed the strainer in the open top of the teapot, "has affected your memory. I've been right here for two years. You're the one who ran away."

"I *went* away," he corrected her quietly. He really wanted to shout it, but he was trying to maintain her level of neutrality. "There's a difference."

"Really." She reached into another cupboard and brought down a package of napkins. "It didn't feel like it to me."

He was suddenly tired of neutrality. "Does that mean you missed me?" he asked.

She took two napkins out of the pack, placed them near the mugs, then tossed the package back up into the cupboard. "I thought I would die," she said with a detachment that belied the words. "Then, after a couple of months, I got word through Nancy via Jave that your hotel job was finished, but you weren't coming home, you were moving on to yet another one, and whatever I felt for you died right there. I knew you were…gone.''

He felt a curious pain from the base of his throat to the pit of his stomach, almost as though he'd swallowed something lethal. It occurred to him grimly that the truth could be hard to swallow.

But it hadn't been his fault. It had been hers. And he wanted to be sure she accepted that.

''I suppose that's a good thing,'' he said, ''because what I felt for you died when you slammed the door on me.''

She turned to look at him then, gray eyes calm. But when she met his gaze, he saw something frantic in hers, something he remembered from the disastrous night when they'd started to make love.

The teakettle whistled, filling the room abruptly with its shrill noise. She looked away, turned the knob off above the burner, then picked up the kettle and poured steaming water over the tea in the strainer.

''Well aren't we lucky, then?'' she asked, her eyes on her task as water filtered slowly through the aromatic leaves. ''This is a good place for us to be. Sexual tension out of the way. Nothing to interfere with the efficient administration of business.''

He struggled to retain his handle on the situation. ''Business?''

''Yes.'' She removed the strainer and put the lid on the teapot. With a hand cupped under the strainer, she carried it to the sink and placed it on the cup. She dried her hand on a towel and gave him that smile again, only this time it was a little warmer, almost friendly. And curiously, that hurt even worse.

''While you slept,'' she said, putting the pot and mugs on a tray, ''I looked over your proposals for the barn. I think I'd be a fool to reject the quality I know you would put into the work for an old grievance over something that's now deader than a doornail. That is, if you think you can work for me?"

"The way it works," he said amiably, "is that we decide together what you want, then I work for me."

"I see." She added the napkins to the tray. "Well, if I wasn't familiar with your work, I might consider your attitude uppity. But, all right. Can you work for yourself on *my* barn?"

He knew it would be safer to cut and run, but he'd never done that in his life, despite what she thought. So he nodded. "Sure I can," he said.

"Good." She picked up the tray and headed for the door. "Come with me," she said. "I'll show you where you'll sleep tonight."

He followed her up a narrow back stairway that led from the kitchen into an upstairs corridor. A pretty pot of eucalyptus stood on a little table against one wall.

He took a rough count of six rooms that opened off the hallway. Most of them held cribs, bunk beds and a plethora of toys.

"Your mom told me this was a boarding house in the heydays of the canneries." She led the way into a room that had a simple double bed, a dresser and a small round table next to which was placed a rocking chair. She put the tray down on the table. "It's perfect for my purposes. I often have kids overnight on weekends, too, so I really appreciate the space." She pointed to a box on the wall over the bed. "There's an intercom. If you don't feel well during the night, buzz me and I'll call Nate. Meanwhile…" She poured tea into one of the mugs and handed it to him. "This is chamomile. It'll help you sleep. If you feel up to it, we can talk business in the morning.''

She poured tea into the second mug, took one of the napkins and headed for the door with it.

"I'm at the far end of the hall," she said with that pleasant smile, "and the bathroom's across the hall, second door down. There's a Bugs Bunny night-light in it. Can't miss it. Need anything else?''

Tom struggled for equilibrium—and it wasn't physical this time. In the space of five minutes she'd admitted she'd missed him while he was away, told him it was unequivocally over between them, offered him work and now stood in a shadowy room with him, a double bed between them.

Could his life get more complex? he wondered. Then he noticed the neat pile of clothes and shaving bag on the rocking chair. They were his.

"Jave stopped by while you were asleep," Amy explained, "but he didn't want to wake you. Nate called him. He wanted to see for himself that you were okay, and he thought you might appreciate a change of clothes in the morning. He said to tell you you can have a rain check on the dinner invitation."

That was Jave, Tom thought. As much as his hovering irritated the hell out of him, it also often produced just what he needed at just the right moment.

"Well..." Amy went to the door, her mug of tea in hand. "Sleep well. And if you have a problem, call me. See you in the morning."

"Right," he said. Then he added grudgingly but sincerely, "Thank you."

"Sure," she replied lightly, and left the room, closing the door behind her.

He wanted to put a fist through it, but he didn't. His

emotions were turbulent enough to launch the action, but his physical strength at the moment was too uncertain to assure that he could follow through.

How dare she be so coolly removed from the roar of anger and the memory of two lonely years that rode on his shoulders. How dare she be kind and considerate when she'd claimed just a few minutes earlier that his absence had made her want to die. How dare she suggest that they were now in this comfortable place.

He didn't feel comfortable at all. At the moment he felt as though he were half testosterone-fueled fourteen-year-old boy and half deranged psychotic. And he'd finally come home because he thought that after two years of living on his own and learning to be free of the past, he had it together. Ha. Amy had managed to destroy that in him in a matter of minutes.

Tom moved the clothes to the foot of the bed, went to the table, picked up the tea, then sat in the rocker by the window and made himself relax.

He could do this. He could work on her barn because he needed work if he was to get his business going again, and she would be too busy with the children to spend much time getting in his way. And if she could be so relaxed and forget that they'd ever meant anything to each other, then so could he.

He took a sip of tea and gagged the moment the pale brew hit his taste buds. He'd never tasted anything so vile in his life. It reminded him of castor oil with grass in it. It could put you to sleep all right—permanently. He put the mug down on the farthest side of the table, as though its mere presence close by could still gag him.

He leaned his head against the high back of the chair and looked out the window. Somewhere beyond the evergreens that curved in a semicircle behind Amy's barn was Nate and Karma's place.

While he felt grateful that Nate had rushed over in response to Amy's call, he also remembered that it was Nate and Jave's doing that he'd come here in the first place.

While he'd been in Arizona, his mother had written him that Amy had quit the hospital, but that was all she'd said. He hadn't known when he'd read the clipping that Kids & Co. was Amy's place. But Jave and Nate had known. And he was going to see that they paid for the deliberate deception.

AMY AWOKE WITH A START to the sound of a crash. It vibrated in the darkness even as she sat up, and she clutched the blanket to her, her first thought that she had an intruder.

Then her brain awakened sufficiently to remind her that Tom, somewhat of an invalid, was at the other end of the hall.

The certainty that something was wrong sent her flying into the hallway without bothering with a robe.

"Tom?" she called anxiously, running toward his room. "Are you all...?"

"Stop!" he ordered sharply.

She did instinctively, but not before landing in midstride on something that ripped into the pad of her bare foot. She cried out in pain and stumbled against the wall.

Tom was there in a minute, his arm going around her to support her. "You stepped on it?" he asked.

She hopped to redistribute her weight, having no choice but to put her arm around the arm that supported her. "What is *it?*"

"Your pot of eucalyptus," he said in a tone of self-condemnation. "I'm sorry. I was headed for the bathroom, forgot about the little table and crashed into it. Before I could grope for the pot, it fell over."

She felt relief despite the pain in her foot. "Thank goodness. I thought something was wrong with you, that you'd...collapsed or something. Ouch."

He had leaned down to examine her foot and made contact with the injury.

"I'm fine," he said, swinging her up into his arms with a suddenness that startled a little scream out of her. "But I think you're the patient this time. It's a good thing we have a lot of doctor friends."

She laughed nervously. "They probably don't think so. I'm not sure you should be carrying me after what you've just been..."

There was no point in continuing. They'd reached the bathroom.

"Can you get the light?" he asked.

She reached out to the right and flipped the switch.

The pink-and-white room came alive in all its minuscule proportions.

He placed her on her good foot, reached to the towel rack for a bath towel, placed it on the counter, then lifted her onto it.

He bent her leg over her other knee and leaned over her to inspect the sole of her foot.

All the air in her lungs left her in a rush. His large, muscular shoulder covered in a cotton T-shirt was a hairbreadth from her breast, his bare arm rested on her thigh, and her foot was caught in the gentle but sturdy grip of his hand. He wore a natty pair of dark blue, waffle-weave Joe Boxer shorts, and the warm fabric rubbed against the inside of her leg, which dangled over the edge of the counter.

His burned leg was clearly visible with its vivid, puckered scars from thigh to ankle, but remembering his extreme sensitivity to attention on it, Amy tried to concentrate on his hands.

But she found she couldn't focus on anything.

Every place in which her body was in contact with his seemed to develop its own erratic pulse. The very small room closed in even more tightly until it felt as though they'd been placed in a box together and someone was closing the lid.

Amy tried to lean back, but there was nowhere to go. She tipped sideways as one hand ended up in the sink.

"Whoa!" He reached up to steady her, his hand connecting with her bare upper arm. "What are you doing?"

"Sorry," she said, her voice little more than a gasp but sounding very loud in the small space. "I...was trying to move out of your light. But there's no place to go."

"I can see," he said, leaning over her again, apparently suffering none of her claustrophobic anxieties. "This isn't deep, but you've got a little piece of pottery stuck in the ball of your foot. Do you have tweezers?"

She pointed to a basket on the counter across from the sink. It held a brush, comb and makeup odds and ends. "In that plastic makeup bag in the basket."

He leaned over her dangling leg to reach for it, unconsciously steadying himself with a hand on her bent knee. Sensation ran along her thigh and into the heart of her like a small bolt of lightning.

He ran the end of the tweezers under the hot water, then leaned over her again and in one easy pull that pinched removed the splinter of pottery.

He ran a thumb over the spot. "I think that's it. Can you feel anything?"

Oh, yes. She felt a lot, she thought, about to strangle with tension. But she wasn't going to tell him that. "No," she replied. "Feels fine."

"Good. Antiseptic in here?"

He leaned her sideways into his arm as he opened the mirrored door of the medicine cabinet behind her. Her hand closed around the rippled muscle of his shoulder in an instinctive grasp for balance, and she had a sudden, vivid recollection of what it was like to hold him, to be held by him.

Then in an instant he had the tube of cream and the tin of Band-Aids. He closed the cabinet and pushed her upright again with clinical detachment. He handed her the tin. "Want to get one out for me?"

She complied, horrified to find her fingers unsteady. She removed a Band-Aid from the tin and watched it flutter past him to the floor as she lost control of it.

He didn't seem to notice. He removed the top from the tube of antiseptic cream and squeezed out a cold line of white stuff against the ball of her foot.

"That ought to do it." He held his hand up for a Band-Aid.

She ripped the end off one and handed it to him. Then she fumbled the box she held and forty-some Band-Aids fell to the floor.

He teased her with a glance before leaning over her to cover the antiseptic cream with the Band-Aid. "I hope you're more coordinated than this when one of your little kids has an injury. There. Feel better?"

He accompanied the question by grasping her waist through the cotton nightshirt she wore and lifting her off the counter and onto her feet.

Trapped with him between the half-open door and the counter in the already narrow space between tub and sink, she was an inch from him and completely flustered by his sexily rumpled appearance in shorts and T-shirt, and his competent ministrations.

She looked up into his eyes and saw the dark flare there as he caught the awareness from her as though it were a germ. But it didn't seem to upset him. It seemed to steady him even further. His eyes held hers without reflecting any of the fluster that was rendering her completely useless.

"I'm fine," she said, and turned, anxious to escape.

"Watch it!" Tom warned, but not before she'd collided with the half-open door.

"Damn it," she muttered as she rubbed her forehead. She'd done the same thing in Jave's office the first time she'd met Tom, only with considerably more dire results. They'd had to put her in a wheelchair and take her to Emergency, where ten stitches had been sewn in her scalp.

She remembered how she'd felt when she'd first looked into his eyes—as though she'd come home after a long and trying day. Only her home had never held that degree of comfort for her. She'd never really felt the sense of belonging she'd experienced when Tom looked back at her and smiled.

Then Tom had offered her a spur-of-the-moment invitation to his birthday party and their rocky relationship had begun.

For a moment, the anger she always felt over the waste of what had seemed so promising dissolved in the memory of how wonderful it had sometimes been.

Tom took her face in his hands and tipped it up to the light, combing her hair aside with his fingers to inspect her forehead. He shook his head over her. "You're going to have a lump there. Come on. I'll get you some ice."

"No." She pushed out of his arms. "I don't want ice. I'll be fine." She slapped the door aside and would have stepped out into the hallway if Tom hadn't caught the back of her nightshirt in his fist and prevented her.

"What?" she demanded testily.

"The hallway is full of broken pottery," he reminded her patiently, "and your feet are still bare." In the narrow space, he cinched an arm around her waist, held her to him and lifted her off her feet. He walked gingerly with her over the rubble and into her room.

Expecting to be set down, she was surprised when he swung her up into his arms as he crossed to her bed and deposited her in the middle of it.

"Thank you," she said stiffly, trying to tug down on the nightshirt that had risen uncomfortably high in the process.

"You're welcome," he said. He placed one hand on the mattress on the other side of her, trapping her under the barrier of his braced arm. "Small payment for the dinner and the accommodations, not to mention your call to Nate."

She tried to back farther into her pillows. He'd had a curious alteration of mood, and she was in no emotional condition at the moment to handle it.

"Anyone would have done the same thing," she said breathlessly.

He leaned a little closer. "But *you* did it. After telling me you no longer care."

"I don't."

"Really?"

"Really."

"Then how come you can't breathe?"

"Because you're leaning on me."

"No. I'm not touching you."

Wasn't he? She took a moment to conduct a sensory examination of her body and it was true; he wasn't touching her. It just felt like he was. Or she could imagine he was. Or maybe…wished that he was.

"Is there something else you want?" she asked, using the defensive tone of her voice to counteract the softening inside her.

"I was going to ask you that," he replied softly.

She didn't know as much about herself as she'd thought, she realized, when two years of rebuilding a life could be undermined and nearly negated by a simple question from the man who'd caused her destruction in the first place.

She could put her arms around him now, she knew, and get back everything that she'd had before he left Heron Point. Then it occurred to her that she hadn't had as much as she'd thought if he'd been able to walk away—and stay away for two years.

"I'd like to go to sleep," she said.

Silence rang between them for a long moment, then he leaned over her and she felt her heart slam against her ribs, thinking he was going to kiss her—ecstatic that he was going to kiss her.

But he simply kissed her forehead and pushed himself off the bed. "Good night, Amy," he said, and left the room.

Through her closed door and above the thumping of her pulse, she heard him go downstairs, rummage around, then return, apparently with a broom.

There was a quiet stirring in the hallway while he swept up, then the closing of a door.

The closing of a door. That felt alarmingly significant as she lay alone in the darkness.

She glanced at the clock on her bedside table. It was 2:32 a.m. Her life had been turned upside down in less than twelve hours.

Everything she'd thought resolved within herself had been dug up and turned over like space for a garden. The question was, would it safely remain fallow, or would something grow?

She turned over and pulled the blanket up under her chin. That was just a fancy metaphor for unearthing a relationship that had brought her nothing but trouble.

No. She wasn't going to do it. She'd fallen under the spell of troubled brown eyes and a sweet and funny manner before, and where had it gotten her? Alone, that's where.

Well, she was smarter this time. This time she owned a house and a business, and had many little lives dependent upon her remaining sane and self-confident.

So Tom Nicholas could just get the hell out of her life.

Except that she'd hired him to renovate her barn. Well, that was all right. He would do fine work and for a better price than anyone else she'd consulted.

It would be a business relationship. They'd agreed upon that earlier. And she'd hold him to it.

Down the hall, Tom climbed back into bed with an unsettling sensation stirring in the pit of his gut—and in his groin. He still had strong feelings for Amy Brown, and she'd just closed another door in his face— at least, metaphorically speaking.

Well. He'd be damned if he'd walk away a second time.

Chapter Four

Tom groaned when he awoke to find Jave leaning over him, taking his pulse.

"Will you give me a *break?*" Tom demanded, trying to yank his wrist away, but Jave shushed him and held fast, his eyes on his watch.

Jave finally dropped Tom's wrist and frowned down at him. "Headache?"

Tom sat up and felt a subtle little throb behind his eyes. "No," he lied. If he'd said yes, he was sure he'd have found himself in intensive care.

"Nausea?"

"No."

"Clear vision?"

"No," Tom answered testily; throwing the blankets back. "You're in sight."

Jave grinned dryly. "Hmm. Irritability. But with you that's a character trait and not a symptom."

Tom stood and squared off with his brother. "I thought we had a talk yesterday about you and Nate staying the hell out of my life?"

"Yeah?"

"Yeah. So Nate gave me this clipping while you pretended to mind your business—which, incidentally, I didn't believe for a minute—and I answered the ad to find myself at Amy's house!"

"We thought you needed work." Jave frowned, as though surprised by his indignation. "And Amy tells me you've struck a deal over the barn. So what's the problem?"

"So the problem is that you knew how things were between me and Amy when I left here."

"Did you?"

Tom stared at him blankly for a minute. "Are we having the same conversation here? Did I know what?"

"How things were between you and Amy," Jave replied calmly. That was one of his favorite tricks. He drove Tom to the edge of apoplexy, but remained calm himself. Someday Tom was going to turn the tables on him and remain calm himself.

Someday. But not today.

"Would you get out so I can get dressed?" Tom asked, taking Jave's arm and leading him to the door. "Thank you for bringing my stuff last night, but don't think for a minute that that gets you off the hook about the clipping. I'll get even."

Jave made a scornful sound. "You've been threatening that for thirty-four years, and by my calculations, you could live to be ninety-two and I'll still be way ahead."

"Goodbye."

Jave handed him a ring with one key on it. He recognized it instantly. It started the *Mud Hen*, the late-twenties cabin cruiser he and Jave had bought together two summers ago. It had been an old bucket at the time, but he'd refinished it inside and Jave and Nancy had honeymooned on it. He'd given Jave his key for safekeeping before he'd left for Arizona.

"In case you want to check it out. There're Cokes in the fridge. We'll expect you for dinner tonight. You can bring the wine."

Jave started for the stairs.

Tom stopped him in the hallway with a shout. "Hey!" He leaned a shoulder in the doorway. "Did I tell you it was good to see you?"

Jave looked back at him with an irrepressible grin. Behind it, Tom saw welcome and the stalwart affection that had seen him through most of his life. "No, but it was pretty obvious when you told me to get out. Incidentally, I just dropped your niece off. You might give her a little attention when you get downstairs. See you tonight."

AMY WAS IN THE KITCHEN on a cordless phone when Tom got downstairs, showered, dressed and feeling like himself again. The shower had done a lot to clear his head.

Bright sunlight poured in through long windows in the living room and onto the three occupants of a nylon mesh playpen in the middle of the room. One of them played with a plastic ball, another swung a string of four large plastic beads against the side of the playpen, and the third watched the television where a tall man in a propeller beanie talked about the alphabet.

The toddlers were all dressed in long-sleeved T-shirts and rompers, and Tom found it difficult to determine gender. As he recalled, one of the three babies born on that same day in September had been a boy.

Amy put her hand over the telephone's mouthpiece. "I'll get your breakfast in a minute. Darcy's mother just put me on hold."

He shook his head. "Thanks, but you don't..."

"I want to talk about the barn," she insisted, holding a finger up as a sign to him that she was about to resume her phone conversation. She held one hand to her ear and walked back into the kitchen.

Prepared to wait, he went to the playpen and knelt down beside it to study the children. They all came to the side, like little colts at the sight of hay.

Which one, he wondered, was Malia?

"Malia?" he asked.

All three looked at him with wide eyes, but he noticed no significant response to the name. He looked for family identification. Malia wasn't Jave's flesh and blood, but she was Nancy's. He looked for brown eyes and brown hair.

Two of the babies had brown hair and one was bald. Three pairs of brown eyes looked back at him.

He put his finger to the cheek of the little baldy.

"Hi," he said. "Are you Malia?"

No, I'm Chelsea. Who are you? You look familiar.

"If you are Malia, I'm your Uncle Tom. And no jokes about Uncle Tom's Cabin, okay? Pete and Eddy have already worn that one out."

Say, what? You had a bad fall yesterday, didn't you? I heard about it. Maybe you should lie down. Want to hold this for a minute? I understand you saved it for me. Thanks!

Tom found a little square of threadbare blanket pushed into his face. He recognized the blanket he'd rescued and so identified its owner. "Ah. You're Chelsea."

Told ya!

"Thank you. What about you?" He turned his attention to the baby with the beads. "Are you Malia?"

Look, dude, the name's Garrett. Do I look like a girl? I know the clothes aren't exactly from the Gap, but hey, I don't have a lot to say about my wardrobe yet, you know what I mean?

Tom pinched a pointy little chin. "You're a pretty little thing."

Oh, yeah? Well, let's put a dimple in yours!

Tom leaned back just in time to avoid the sudden fling of the plastic beads in his face. He went to the third baby, who was trying to climb out of the pen.

Hey, unc! It's me! I'm Malia. Over here.

"Okay, it's got to be you." Tom unhooked the little leg now stuck on the edge of the pen and lifted the toddler into his arms. "Malia?"

She laughed and patted his shoulder. "Lia!" she said.

Feeling as though he'd accomplished something truly brilliant, Tom grinned at her. "Well, how are you? You were just a fingerling when I left here. Bet your brothers have been spoiling you."

She watched him with a broad grin, apparently as fascinated with him as he was with her. She launched into a barrage of sounds.

Yeah, they're cool! How are you? Everybody was worried about you. I don't know why. You look fine to me. Want to watch this with me? It's all about letters. You know, A, B, C…that stuff. I have to know that, 'cause my mom's a writer, and when we work at the computer, she always makes a file for me. She says someday I'll put a story there. Look. A is for alligator. B is for…

Malia, suddenly bored with him, turned her attention to the television. He put her back in the playpen, and she hung her arms over the side closest to the TV and watched.

"Isn't she precious?" Amy asked from the edge of the fireplace. "We're all convinced Heron Point was blessed the day these three were born. Jave's boys have really become a pair of ladies' men. They're going to be even more handsome than the two of you."

He raised an eyebrow at the compliment. Her cheeks pinked as though that admission embarrassed her. "Well, let's face it," she said finally, as though trying to slough off her discomfort with candor. "We both know that good looks were never your problem."

He shrugged, wondering how to explain without sounding falsely modest that it was something he never gave much thought to. But he did like the notion that *she* thought about his looks—and liked them.

She studied him, her eyes...wistful?

"I know. And your ignorance of it was always part of your mystique. Come on. I've got your breakfast."

"I have a mystique?" he asked in amusement, following her into the kitchen.

"Everyone has a mystique," she replied, pointing him to a place at the table where she'd already placed a glass of juice and a cup of coffee. She took a plate out of the oven and placed it in front of him. Then she pulled a little folding gate closed that separated the kitchen from the living room. She was on one side, he on the other.

She pointed to the coffeemaker on the counter. "Help yourself to more. Kate should be here in fifteen minutes. When you're finished we can talk about the barn."

Then she disappeared around the fireplace, and he heard the immediate scamper of little feet in all directions as she apparently released the trio from their nylon prison.

While Tom ate, two more little children were delivered to Kids & Co. by mothers in a hurry. Tom watched the doorway into the living room with mild trepidation. One child pedaled by on a little plastic trike, another went by pulling a toy, one was waving wildly with a plastic wand that produced bubbles, and Malia, a stuffed dog hanging from her hand by its tail, peered in over the gate and grinned.

"Hi, Malia," he called, waving his fork at her.

She waved back, then ran away with a shriek of laughter.

Kate arrived on time and launched into immediate action as the toddler on the trike tried to extend his tour of the living room to include the great outdoors.

Amy appeared on the other side of the gate and looked at his empty plate. "More toast?" she asked.

He shook his head, thinking she looked like something a man could nibble on this morning in slim black pants and a red, white and black plaid shirt. Her hair was tied back with a narrow length of red ribbon. "Thanks, that was plenty," he said, carrying his plate to the sink. "I've done nothing for the past four days to burn up energy."

"You ready to look at the barn?" She waved the sheet of paper with his proposals. "I have your suggestions, but I also have a few questions."

"Can you get away with all that activity going on out there?"

She laughed. "This is a good time—while Kate's still fresh, and before we serve snacks."

The baby on the trike went pedaling by the doorway at Olympic-competition speed. Tom shook his head as Amy stepped over the gate. "I guess I thought it would be more organized. You know—games, lessons, group things."

She went to the back door and opened it. Birdsong and sunshine flowed over her. "We try to do that with the bigger kids who come after school, but these guys are still too small for that. The best we can do for them is make them feel happy and at home and let them do their own thing and make their own discoveries."

He followed her out the door. "But they're all going in different directions. How do you keep up?"

"You just don't do anything else. You watch them every minute, keep their tummies fed and their toys running and they're happy."

The morning was glorious, the field green and fragrant after yesterday's rain, the Douglas firs a jagged backdrop to the bright blue sky filled with tufty white clouds. In another few weeks those clouds would bring incessant rain, but this morning they were simply a beautiful accent in a picture-postcard landscape.

Nestled in the crescent-shaped line of trees, the ramshackle barn stood in faded splendor, a remnant of another time.

"I think I would have liked to be here when the barn was operational," she said as they strode toward it, side by side. She seemed perfectly relaxed this morning, as though she didn't remember their middle-of-the-night encounter.

He did. He hadn't gotten to sleep for hours. He hadn't been sure if it was sexual frustration or extreme irritation. He still didn't know. But on a day like this, it was hard to feel negatively about anything, so he made himself put it aside.

He helped Amy push through the big double doors and into the musty space poorly lit by one overhead light on the far side.

"I think the previous tenant used this half of the barn

for storage," Amy said, "so they weren't concerned with how well lit it was. You can do electrical work, can't you?"

"Yes."

"Good. I'd like to use this side for an indoor playground. Swings, slides, all the stuff that's outside, but I'll put mats all around it. The kids really miss the swing set when it's raining."

She walked into the lit half of the room. "This I'd like to set up just like a living room with another TV, sofas and chairs, and maybe even a little library in a corner. I have one little girl who comes on Mondays and Fridays and she actually tries to do her homework with the music blaring and the babies crawling over her."

"Sectioning off a space would be no problem."

"Good." She stepped back to point up at the loft. "I really liked your idea about making an office out of the loft. I was up there once the day I bought the place, but I hadn't even thought about actually using it. Right now I do all my paperwork at the kitchen table or sitting on my bed. But...is the ceiling really high enough? I seem to remember I was ducking the whole time I was up there."

Tom headed for the ladder. "Come on," he said. "I'll show you." He turned before he began to climb to see that she still stood in the middle of the room, looking a little sheepish. "What?" he asked.

She went toward him with obvious reluctance. "I remember that I didn't like that ladder. It's so...perpendicular."

He nodded. "It's a ladder. They tend to be that way."

She scolded him with a look. "I know that. I'm just

accustomed to going upstairs on nice solid steps, not little flimsy sticks.''

"Well, you can trust me that it's high enough, but if you come up with me I can show you exactly what I had in mind." He beckoned her. "I'll be just a rung below you. It'll be physically impossible for you to fall.''

Amy suspected it was a bad idea, but something perverse inside her wouldn't let her say no. The night before had proved that their attraction for each other was still incendiary, but the new and improved Amy had chosen to put her fears aside. She wasn't going to deprive herself of taking part in the planning of her office just because she used to have a thing for this man.

She pocketed the sheet of paper that held his proposal and went to the ladder. She held the sides and stepped up a rung.

He came up right behind her, his body paralleling hers exactly. The extra inches he had on her were just about the distance from rung to rung. His mouth was right at her ear.

"Just go slowly," he said. "It's only about a dozen rungs.''

She counted them, feeling him right behind her, a wall of security and yet a six-foot-plus memory she was determined not to relive.

But when he was being solicitous like this, when he was being tolerant of her shortcomings and quirks and not making her feel inadequate as her family tended to, she felt drawn to him, could almost feel the inclination of her body into his arms even against her will.

She was imagining things, she told herself, because he was so close behind her. Their bodies bumped lightly, her arm against his hand, her head against his shoulder, her hip against his belt buckle. Suspended on the rickety ladder near the shadowed loft still redolent of hay after all these years, Amy felt as though the innocent little touches took on a drama that she fought against with all the forward-driving impetus of her new resolve.

She didn't realize she had stopped until Tom asked, his breath warm against her cheek, "You okay? One more step and you'll be able to see into the loft."

That did it for her. If he was unaware of the tension, it must be an atmosphere she was creating herself out of old dreams and a misbegotten fling. She climbed the rest of the way up, scrambled onto her knees at the top and waited, arms folded over her chest, for him to join her.

Aware that she was breathing rapidly, she strode away from him as he cleared the top of the ladder and stepped off. It was simple exertion, but she didn't want him thinking it was something else.

She went to the open hay doors. Her breathing slowed, and she sat on the wide sill of the opening and looked out, thinking it would be wonderful to be able to work up here and look out at the children at play on the swing set or, when they'd all gone home, to work on the book she had in mind and be able to look out at the moon and the stars and the river visible over the treetops of residential Heron Point.

Tom sat facing her, his legs stretched out over hers, which were folded daintily to her side.

"Wonderful view," he said, letting his eyes scan the panorama. "You can see what's playing at the Liberty from here."

She turned her head to look. "You cannot," she denied in a tone that berated him for exaggerating.

"Well, if I had an office up here," he said, ignoring the reproof, "I'd keep the binoculars handy. You'd be able to keep an eye on Rodney's dad at the port."

"I let his wife do that."

He ignored her and went on. "You can watch Nate and Karma coming and going, you can watch the kids walking over here after school. Hmm. If we had that mountain ash cut down, you could probably even see the high school."

"Why would I want to see the high school? Those kids are watching *each other* after school."

"Well. You might want to see if Principal Fuller employs the same technique on single lady teachers that he uses on you."

She rolled her eyes. "What technique?"

"The heroic single father technique. The 'I don't know what I'd do without you' technique. And that's usually accompanied by an adoring look into your eyes, and the close scrutiny of your backside when you turn away."

She gasped, half indignant, half amused. The notion was so preposterous. "He doesn't do that!"

"How do you know? Do you have eyes in the back of your head?"

"As a matter of fact, I do. Anyone who cares for children does. Steve Fuller isn't interested in my backside."

"I saw him look."

"You'd had a blow to the head. And so what if he did look? I've noticed that he fills out a pair of Dockers very nicely."

Tom knew that his stunned expression had to look comical. How Amy had changed. The shy little klutz he'd fallen in love with was becoming a woman of the world—well, of as much of the world as was visible in Heron Point.

"Amaryllis Brown!" he said, unable to hold back the grin. "You hussy."

She hadn't become sophisticated enough to hold back a blush, however. She held her head high, unwilling to appear repentant for her admission, but her cheeks were pink.

"Grow up, Nicholas. The new millennium is coming. We're taking men on dates now."

"And how many men have you squired around town?" he teased.

She lifted a haughty shoulder. "Dozens."

"It doesn't count if they're under eight."

"We're not here to talk about my conquests," she said, "we're here to plan an office." She looked out at the view and sighed, a little smile curving her lips. "I'd like to put my desk right here. Can we glass this in?"

He congratulated himself on having just the right answer for her. "Not only can we glass it in," he said, "but it just so happens that in my warehouse of scrounged materials, I have a window that I think would fit here. It's framed in leaded stained glass squares with clear glass in the center, so you can have beauty but keep your view."

"It sounds perfect." She stood suddenly and wandered across the loft. "I suppose an old-fashioned railing with turned balusters would be a fortune."

"Yeah, it would," he admitted, following her. "If I could scrounge some, it would be less, but I'd need the time to look."

"Of course." She was becoming businesslike again. He wanted to call back those few minutes at the window that reminded him of the slightly combative companionship they'd once shared, but it couldn't be forced, and she was apparently on another track.

He shouldn't be surprised. Even in the good times two years ago she'd been high-strung and changeable.

"What kind of a mood do you want up here?" he asked. "Rustic, nautical, feminine?"

She looked around, her eyes losing focus as she thought about finally having her own work space. "I wish there was such a thing as feminine nautical," she said. "You know. Sort of...ship's-plank walls, but decorated with flowers and stuff instead of brassy ship's wheels and barometers." Then she focused on him. "You know what I mean?"

He was grinning. "Not a clue," he admitted frankly. "But you tell me what you want for walls, I'll put it up, and the 'flowers and stuff' is your responsibility."

"Right." She looked at all the open beams above her head. "It's all in good shape, right? No rot or bugs or anything?"

"No signs that I can see. You do have some rotten windows downstairs, though, that should be replaced."

She tapped a foot on the floor. "And this is good and solid?"

"Very."

"Good." She made a shoulders-up gesture of pleasure that brought the best times of the past back like the stroke of silk across his mind. It felt wonderful for a moment, then it was gone, leaving him with a sense of loss.

"There's good energy up here," she said, looking around again with that pleased expression. "Like happy ghosts still live here or something."

He tried to relate to her fanciful shift in mood. "Well, that's not surprising," he said. "This was probably a rendezvous spot in the old days for the farmer's daughter and some poor hand on a fishing boat who wasn't considered good enough for her.''

She appeared to like the notion. She walked to the wall of the barn and back as though expecting to find them in a mad embrace in the corner.

Then she looked at him with a surprised smile. "And what kind of binoculars did you have for that particular vision?''

"I'm basically full of bull,'' he replied. "Always have been.''

"Not bull,'' she corrected him, coming back toward him. "Imagination. I used to like that about you. You were always more...connected to your environment than men usually are. If they like the outdoors, it's because they like to hunt and fish in it, take something from it. You just liked it—'' she hesitated, then finished the sentence in a quick, quiet rush, as though regretting that she'd begun the explanation "—because it was there.''

She stopped a foot away from him, folded her arms, then unfolded them in a fluster.

He didn't dare smile. But he tucked away for future consideration the memory of the flush in her cheeks and the watchful little glow in her eyes. He suspected she wasn't as comfortable with their situation as she claimed to be. Considering he was in a total flap, he appreciated that glimpse of truth.

"See?'' he said.

Amy, lost in her loose-lipped admission that she'd liked certain things about him, tried to get herself together and restore a certain employer-employee relationship to this discussion.

"See what?'' she asked flatly, thinking he meant,

"See? Your behavior proves you still have feelings for me" or "See? All I have to do is get close to you and you begin to dither."

When he said neither of those things, but simply pointed overhead, she felt disoriented, confused.

"Lots of headroom," he clarified for her. "You were worried about it, remember?" He ran a hand between his head and the four or five inches that remained between it and the roof's slope. "Fuller would fit up here easily."

She pursed her lips at him. "Suggesting that he's somehow deficient because he's not as tall as you are?"

He widened his eyes innocently. She knew it was an act. "Not at all. Although I'm not sure he's tall enough to hold you to the ladder to get you up here."

"Well, if you're putting in stairs, that won't be a problem, will it? And even though this is absolutely none of your business, I'll tell you one more time that he does not have designs on me."

"Okay, I'll tell you what," he said. "We'll make a small wager. If he doesn't make a move on you in the next couple of weeks, I'll let you have that leaded-glass window as a gift."

She liked the sound of that. And she knew Steve Fuller. He had loved his wife and he still wasn't over her death. She smiled and held out her hand. "Deal."

But when he reached out to take it, she drew it back, aware suddenly of an unfinished detail. "And I'll owe you for it if I lose—which isn't going to happen, but for the sake of argument we should have all details clear."

He nodded. "Absolutely. Fine with me."

"All right." She extended her hand, somehow feeling as though this was more significant than it seemed, as though thunder should roll, or the wind suddenly howl.

He took it and gave it a firm shake. "Do you have time to go over the downstairs with me?"

She glanced at her watch. "Can we do it in fifteen minutes?"

"I think so. Unless you have questions."

Getting on the ladder from above was much more difficult than getting off of it had been. She couldn't see behind her and had the most unsettling sensation of stepping out into space.

But Tom took a firm hold of her ankle and placed her foot on a rung. "Okay," he directed, "just slip your other leg down between me and the ladder and we've got it made."

She made herself comply, though she didn't want to at all. The combination of his closeness and her dislike of the ladder had her nervous and unsure. And the new and improved Amy didn't like that at all.

The moment her feet reached the rung above his, he leaned in, his solidity against her managing to be comforting as well as unsettling. "Okay?" he asked.

"Yeah," she lied breathlessly.

"Good. Here we go."

Because they were going down, his progress placed him two rungs lower, and now she could feel his chin bump against her back, her hips strike his shoulder. At one point she felt her balance shift, kicked out anxiously and got him in the stomach.

She heard his "Ooof!" of surprise, and embarrassed, she groaned an apology.

He laughed. "It's okay. Just keep coming."

She followed his instructions, then suddenly hands

nipped her waist and she was swung to the concrete floor.

She let herself sag against him in relief. Then, realizing what she'd done, she straightened and pulled at the hem of her shirt.

"Thank you," she said, pulling the shreds of her dignity together. "Maybe you could put the stairs in first thing. Show me the bad windows."

Tom followed her across the room, a hand rubbing at his chest, against which her round bottom had bumped several times, and thought he'd leave construction of the stairs till the last possible moment.

Chapter Five

Tom stepped aboard the *Mud Hen* for the first time in two years and went to the afterdeck to simply stand there and absorb the sense of rightness he always felt on the river.

Years ago—another lifetime ago—when he and Jave had bought their first boat, a fifty-foot Fiberglas vessel called the *River Lady*, together, he had just been made battalion chief, and Jave was the new head of Radiology at Riverview. They'd both been cocky, had felt like they were living the American dream and that they deserved it because they'd worked hard and followed all the rules.

Then Jave's first wife had left him and the boys, Tom and his men had responded to the fire in the hotel, Davey had died, and Tom had spent three months in the hospital recovering from a broken leg and third-degree burns from hip to foot.

He and Jave had both needed money, so they'd sold the *River Lady*.

It had taken almost two years, but they'd both gotten on their feet again and they'd responded to an ad in the classifieds that had brought them to the *Mud Hen*. It had been in terrible shape, but had an energy Tom had felt even then.

He remembered touching the lapstrake hull and being aware of how different he was from the younger man who'd bought a share in the *River Lady.* Then, untried and flush with a little success, he'd looked for cosmetic beauty and speed.

When he'd first seen the *Mud Hen,* he'd related instantly to its worn and wounded appearance. He'd felt just like that for so long.

Jave had kicked in his share just to humor him, he was sure. The old sea dog who'd sold it to them had been repairing a hole in the deck and was having her painted when they bought it. But Tom had spent every spare moment he had on the inside, and now the *Mud Hen* was a cleaner, more finished boat that had been through a lot and endured and prevailed, and was now ready to hit the open sea again.

Like him.

He went down into the galley, found the Cokes Jave had told him would be there and wandered into the blue-and-gray stateroom.

He sat on a corner of the bed, downed a long swig of cola and felt old needs begin to prowl through his body.

He ran a hand through his hair and groaned, knowing there was nothing he could do about it. Over the past two years he'd had sex carefully but casually and endured various reactions to his scarred and puckered leg.

He didn't know why he'd been able to deal with the touch of virtual strangers when he'd made such a scene when Amy had placed a hand on it. He'd guessed it had been because Arizona wasn't home to him—it was a sort of limbo where he held his real life at bay while he tried to deal with who he was and what he was going to do.

It had been a little like being touched in a dream.

But the dream was over. He was home, and this was where he intended to stay.

And he didn't want to have sex with just any woman. His body craved Amy.

He wasn't sure why. He was still angry over her re-action when he'd told her he had to leave, though he saw interest in her eyes now when she looked at him. But they'd both been there before.

They seemed to be able to identify qualities in each other they needed, without seeming to be able to reach them. She'd come to Heron Point to escape her family and a part of herself she'd said she'd been unhappy with. And his life had been so confused the past few years that he hardly knew up from down.

But he was home to fix that. And she was on a new track. Was this a second chance? It was hard to tell. She seemed drawn to him one minute and then ran away from him the next.

And he still wasn't sure how he felt, except to know for certain that he wasn't indifferent. He felt the same sexual attraction he'd experienced two years ago, but emotionally there was a lot of old stuff between them still unresolved.

He hated that.

He placed the pop can on the small strip of deck between the berth and the bulkhead, then lay back and closed his eyes.

Maybe he'd been a pirate in another life. That might explain his love of boats and the deep-down wish that a winsome woman could be kidnapped into a man's life and held there by sexual prowess and pretty baubles traded from the Orient.

As far as he was concerned, he thought sleepily, it beat the current system hands down for finding a woman.

"AMY! TRUMAN'S PICKING ON me again!"

Darcy's shrieking voice brought Amy from the kitchen where she was unloading the dishwasher. Because all the babies had been retrieved earlier in the afternoon, Amy had let Kate go home early. Rodney's father had just picked him up, so she was alone with the two warring factions.

"Well, it's stupid," Truman said in his own defense, "for her to play with a doll she never takes out of the box. Now she's got clothes for it that aren't going to come out of the package, either? Give me a break!"

Darcy held her precious packages to her, her eyes wide with hurt and brimming with tears. "I *want* to take them out of the box, but then they won't be worth anything."

"Truman, we've been over this," Amy said, putting an arm around each of them. "The doll is hers. That means she can do what she wants to with it."

"But, it's dumb to…" Truman began.

"To Darcy," Amy interrupted, "it makes sense. And since it's hers, that's all that matters. So butt out, okay?"

"You break everything," Darcy accused Truman. "You can't keep anything nice."

"Well, I wouldn't keep it in a box, that's for sure. What's the good of having something you can't play with?"

"You can't play with it if you break it, either!" she shot back.

A knock on the front door saved Amy from having to find some wise advice with which to end the confrontation. And she was grateful for that because she couldn't think of a thing.

Darcy and Truman were as opposite as two children could be, and not simply because of their gender. He was rowdy and explosive but deep-down sweet. She was introspective and moody and seemed afraid to have fun.

Truman did break almost everything he touched, but Amy guessed it was a simple problem common to many boys his age—strength outdistancing finesse. But his might have been compounded by anger over his mother's death that exaggerated his naturally impulsive personality.

Darcy, on the other hand, spent weekends with her grandmother while her mother worked a second job, and seemed obsessed with her mother's financial difficulties.

The doll and then the clothes that she'd arrived with that morning had been gifts from her father. Amy didn't know if the notion of "saving" the doll until it appreciated had been passed on by Darcy's mother or grandmother, or if Darcy had simply overheard something and imposed this decision on herself.

Either way, the other children had given her a lot of grief over it. And the way she carried it around rather than leaving it on a shelf was proof that she loved it, and that was what disturbed Amy. The child had to be hating the thought that she had to part with it one day.

Amy opened the door to Ginger Billings, Darcy's mother. She was small and harried-looking, and always seemed preoccupied.

But when Darcy ran tearfully into her arms, Amy saw all the mother-instincts come to the fore. She wrapped the child in her embrace and held her close, asking for an explanation. When Darcy wept instead of providing it, Truman admitted grudgingly that he'd teased her about the doll. Then he braced himself, as though expecting her wrath.

Instead, she gave him a sad look that made him shift uncomfortably.

"Her father sent it for her birthday," she explained, rocking Darcy gently back and forth. "And my mom doesn't like him because he never sends money to help me, so she told Darcy if she loved me she wouldn't play with it, she'd save it and sell it when it became valuable." She hugged Darcy more tightly and kissed the top of her head. "So that's what she's doing. I've told her it would make me happier if she took it out of the box and played with it, but she's trying to help with the money."

Her eyes were now filled with tears. She reached a hand out to Truman and cupped his chin. "Please don't tease her about it."

Truman looked at Amy, his eyes wide and horrified. "I'm sorry," he said. "I won't anymore."

Ginger turned to leave, Darcy still holding on to her, and almost collided with Steve Fuller, who stood just inside the door and had probably heard the discussion.

They studied each other uncertainly, then Ginger pulled the door closed behind her.

"Did I hear that you were picking on that little girl?" Steve asked Truman, his expression displeased.

"I don't think he was picking on her," Amy interceded, "as much as having trouble understanding her behavior." She ruffled Truman's hair, knowing he hadn't been malicious. "He's a very practical boy. He didn't understand why she wouldn't unwrap her toy and play with it."

Steve nodded, still frowning at Truman. "Well, now that you do, you'll leave her alone about it, right?"

"Yeah. But isn't it weird to tell a kid not to play with it?"

Steve nodded. "I think so. But it's something her mom has to deal with, Truman, not you."

"Yeah." Truman heaved a sigh and went to the coat closet for his jacket. "I thought she was gonna yell at me," he said as they walked to the door. "But she was really nice. How come you're here so early, Dad?"

"Computer's down. I thought we'd take advantage of it and go to dinner and to the movies." Steve smiled at Amy. "I don't suppose you're free to come with us."

Oh, God. There went her leaded-glass window. Or did an invitation to go out actually constitute "a move"? She wasn't sure. Men had such strange euphemisms for the steps in a relationship.

She looked into Steve's expectant gaze and could find nothing sexual in it. It appeared to be a simple friend-to-friend invitation. And certainly if an invitation did constitute "a move," the definition would change if a child was included.

"Thanks," she said, "but I have a million things to do tonight. Unfortunately, my duties don't end when the last child goes home."

"Sure." He did seem disappointed, but that might just be good manners. "See you tomorrow night."

"And don't forget she has that book-party thing tomorrow," Truman reminded. "Mrs. Nicholas talked about it when she picked up Malia."

"That's right." Steve opened the door, and they all

stepped out onto the porch. "I'm invited also. Fortunately, Truman has a Cub Scout meeting."

Amy walked them down the steps. "I didn't know you knew Jave and Nancy."

"I met Nancy when she came to school to help with Career Day. Like most former English teachers, I have a novel in the bottom drawer of my desk, too. We got to talking and became friends."

"Anyway..." Steve turned to Amy, who'd stopped on the bottom step. "Want me to pick you up?"

Uh-oh. Another invitation. Though this one didn't include a child, it did involve a host of other people. So that couldn't constitute "a move," either.

But maybe *two* such invitations did?

"Ah...thanks, but Diantha Pennyman and I are going together." She smiled too broadly. It was hard to turn a man down twice in the same evening—move or not. "I'll see you there."

"All right. Good night."

Amy tidied the kitchen, did laundry, straightened and vacuumed, then organized food for the following day's meals.

Then she wandered out to the barn with a cup of tea and stood in the middle of the big shadowy room and looked up. She'd have loved to climb the ladder, but she wasn't sure she'd make it, and caring for little children involved too much running to risk having to do it with a broken leg.

So she simply pushed her visions of an office to the back of her mind and walked around on the lower level and imagined it finished with wallboard and paint, pictured new windows that didn't leak and actually *opened,* envisioned new flooring covered in high-traffic carpeting.

She'd asked Sam at the Secondhand Barn to watch for sturdy furniture in good condition, and she pictured it placed around the room. She saw a little library in the corner.

She sat cross-legged in the middle of the room as darkness began to fall and thought about how far she'd come in two years. Her family had thought she was crazy when she'd left the hospital job her uncle had arranged for her.

She'd only taken it in the first place because it had gotten her out of New York and away from her parents' concern and the glow of her sisters' successes. But the job *had* resulted in her friendships with the parents of the September 23 babies, and she considered them gifts from the hand of providence.

She was grateful that she hadn't fallen on her face in this new endeavor. The children seemed to enjoy coming to her home, and their parents seemed to appreciate her approach to child care. If the addition of the barn did what she thought it would do for her in the winter months, she might consider expanding to Seaside.

She could, if she wanted to dream big, have a chain of child-care facilities.

But that was putting the cart way ahead of the rocking horse. She had to make the barn work first.

She raised her knees and wrapped her arms around them, thinking that the only phase of her life that did not seem to be moving forward was her attraction to Tom. She wanted to be over it.

She admitted to herself with a sigh that she was already anticipating tomorrow, when he would arrive in his truck and go to work. She would be too busy with the children to spend any time with him, but she felt a little glow in the pit of her stomach at the knowledge that he would be here.

That was crazy. She accepted that. But it didn't change the way she felt.

Her mother would probably think that typical of her. "Poor Amy" was the only one of the girls who couldn't focus, Amy had once overheard her telling a friend. "She doesn't have the same drive as the other girls. She tries all kinds of things but she fails at most of them. I don't know what will become of her. And, of course, she's too tall and not very pretty."

"This is it, Mom," she heard herself say aloud, her voice hollow in the cavernous room. "Child-care maven and ill-starred lover. Didn't know I had it in me, did you?"

TOM, JAVE AND NANCY sat in a swing in the backyard of Jave and Nancy's home on the hill overlooking Heron Point. Jave had barbecued salmon for dinner, and they were all replete, the boys playing halfhearted one-on-one basketball with Mo, a large brown-and-black dog of doubtful heritage. The adults had alternated pushing Malia on the swing. She was now in Tom's arms, yawning and rubbing her eyes.

"No, I am not coming to your autograph party tomorrow," Tom said to Nancy, who sat between him and Jave, "because you allowed your husband to set me up to run blindly into Amy."

Nancy leaned into Jave's arm, which rested on the back of the upholstered swing, and raised an eyebrow at Tom. "Allowed? You think he consults me before he takes action on anything?"

"He must," Tom replied, bracing Malia's little body as she fought sleep and stood up on his thighs. "Otherwise I'm sure he'd have made a lot more mistakes than he has.''

"Actually," Nancy said, patting his knee, "he didn't ask my permission, but he did tell me that Nate had the clipping and I must confess that I applauded the plan."

Tom gave her a grimly disapproving look. "I'm appalled."

"Why?" She smiled, apparently unimpressed with his expression. "You'd have been too stubborn to look her up, and she'd have been too proud to come to you and tell you that she's done nothing for two years but think about you."

Tom studied Nancy's face, certain she was lying. But she looked clear-eyed and her gaze didn't waver. "She's worked like a fiend to put Kids & Co. together, but she refuses to date, and all she does when she and Jo and Karma and I go anywhere together is watch the faces of people passing by. It was our theory that she was watching for you to come home."

Malia jumped on his lap. He bracketed her little body with his hands. "Well, I think your theory went down in flames when she took one look at me and told me to leave."

"Pardon me," she said quietly, "but did you miss the part where she hired you to do the barn?"

"She hired me because I'm the best carpenter for a hundred miles."

"Then it's up to you to take the opportunity afforded you to prove to her that you're the best husband material for a hundred miles also."

Tom turned his attention to Malia. "I'm beginning to think your mom is as much of a buttinsky as your dad."

"Mommy!" Malia said, pointing at Nancy.

"Right," Tom praised her. "Buttinsky. Mommy is a buttinsky. Can you say that?"

Yeah, but I think I'd get in trouble. What's your problem with Amy, anyway? I saw you watching her this morning when she was playing with us. Daddy watches Mom like that. I think it makes babies. I heard Truman and Rodney talking about it. So, watch out. That playpen Amy puts us in when she's busy is pretty crowded already.

Malia pointed to Jave. "Daddy!" she said.

"Yeah, I know." Tom bumped noses with her. "But why are you so happy about it?"

'Cause he can throw me in the air and he never drops me. He rescues me when the boys play too rough, he knows a lot of cool songs and he loves me a lot. He tells me all the time.

"Who's going to watch the kids while we're all at this party?" Tom asked.

"Beachie," Nancy replied. "We made a deal. She'll miss the party to watch the kids for three autographed books."

Nurse Beacham had been at Riverview as long as Tom could remember. She had a reputation for being the classic no-nonsense autocrat, but underneath was a heart of gold. And there wasn't anything she wouldn't do for Jave—and now Nancy.

"Then I guess I'll come. Who else is going to be there?"

"Most of our friends."

"Amy?"

"She's coming with Diantha. Remember Diantha?"

"Of course. She's pretty unforgettable." Diantha Pennyman ran the health food store next door to Jo Jeffries's Coffee Country. She was also an astrologer, and Tom remembered that she'd worked up a forecast for Jo and Ryan's baby at the time of its birth, and Jo had shared it with Nancy and with Nate's wife, Karma.

"Did her predictions about the Libra babies come to pass?" he asked Nancy.

Yeah! She said I'd have a keen intellect, but it's hard to convince anybody that that's true, because I've only got about fifty words in my vocabulary.

"I'll say," Nancy replied. Malia was now leaning out of Tom's arms toward her, and Nancy took her from him and cradled her in her arms. "She predicted she'd be a finicky eater, and that's right on. She also said she'd be hospitable and compassionate and philanthropic. She isn't really into sharing yet, but I swear she's just like Eddy in that she doesn't know a stranger."

Nancy stopped, then she laughed a little self-consciously and smiled across the yard at the boys, now digging the basketball out of a rhododendron bush. "Not that I should expect her to be anything like either boy. I just forget sometimes that they're not related by blood."

Jave bent the arm he held on the back of the swing, gently caught her neck in the crook of it and looked down at her with an expression so intimate, so grave that Tom felt like an intruder. "They're related by love," Jave said softly. "When we got married, you gave her to me and I gave you the boys. The heart pumps the blood, the blood doesn't pump the heart."

She gave him a smile that said things that made Tom blush.

"All right, I'm out of here." He stood. "Every time I'm around you two, I expect birds carrying silk banners to come by and the mice to start singing. If there's a pumpkin parked behind my truck, I'm reporting you to the DMV."

"It's licensed," Jave said with a grin, standing and taking Malia from Nancy so that she could rise. The boys came running over with Mo bounding behind them.

"How come you're going?" Eddy asked. He was twelve, and Tom swore he'd grown a good six inches since he'd seen him two years ago.

"I can only take so much of your dad," he said, putting an arm around each boy as everyone walked him down the driveway to his truck.

Eddy laughed and grinned at Jave. "I know. Us, too."

Jave swatted at his head and Eddy laughed.

Pete, at nine, was quieter and more serious, though Tom thought he seemed less so since Nancy had come into the boys' lives. "Me and Eddy are gonna bring our basketball to Amy's, and if you take a coffee break in the afternoon when we get there, we can play. She has a hoop in back of the house."

"That might work," Tom said with a wink at Jave. "But we're going to put a library in the barn so you'll have a quiet place to do your homework. Wouldn't you rather do that?"

Both boys frowned up at him. "Maybe," Pete said brightly, "you could talk Amy into changing the plan from a library to a video arcade."

Tom drove home with the sound of family laughter ringing in his ears. Coming home, this part of it, anyway, had been a good idea.

Chapter Six

Amy was out of bed at 5:00 a.m., and showered and dressed and sipping coffee by five-thirty. Children would be arriving by six-thirty, and she treasured the time alone to prepare herself for the day.

When she opened the door to greet her first arrival, Tom's truck was pulling into the driveway.

With a quiet tap of the horn in greeting, he pulled around the back of the house and drove across the field to the barn. The back of the truck was loaded with lumber and tools, and Amy responded with a wave, a sense of excitement stirring in her chest. Kids & Co.'s expansion was officially underway.

She peered out the kitchen window in the middle of the morning while she prepared snacks and felt mild concern when she saw that the truck was gone. Then she heard it turn into the driveway, and as she watched it went bumping across the field, full of more lumber, more tools.

Bless Ryan Jeffries. Chelsea's father was the manager of the bank with some district pull, and he'd gone to bat for her and gotten her the loan that was paying for this.

At lunchtime, she saw Tom sitting outside in the sun,

propped up against the wall, eating a sandwich, a tall thermos beside him.

By afternoon snack break, he was power-washing the barn. All the children who came after school were watching from the backyard, fascinated. They included Pete and Eddy, who didn't give a second thought to running across the field to greet their uncle.

Truman, Rodney and Darcy ran after them, and Kate followed while Amy stayed with the toddlers. She would have liked to go, too, but if Tom was to spend two months at work out there, she had to establish a professional distance from him and maintain it for the sake of her work and his.

By the time he left at five, it looked as though the entire barn had been power-washed.

"My goodness," Amy said, looking out the back door, flanked by his nephews. "He'll be ready to paint tomorrow."

"He has to scrape first," Eddy said.

"I thought the power-washer did that."

"Mostly, but he has to get the stuff it didn't get." He spoke very matter-of-factly. "'Cause he's the best, you know. Nothing gets by him."

She was sure that was true.

"GOOD GRIEF!" DIANTHA exclaimed as the crowd assembled at Booked Solid pressed in around the table where Amy poured champagne and Diantha kept the hors d'oeuvres trays filled. "Murder must be better business than health food."

"Or accounting." Karma Foster, Nate's wife and Garrett's mother, swapped a tray filled with decorated cookies for an empty one. She was dark-haired and pretty, and Amy had always envied her calm control.

"How are the cookies holding up?" Jo Jeffries, who'd taken on the job of catering the affair, held two hot pots of coffee in her arms. She was tall and blond, and always seemed to Amy as though she'd just walked out of a pre-Raphaelite painting. Her hair was wild, her face angelic. She'd been a surrogate mother for Ryan's and her sister Cassie's baby, then married Ryan after her sister was killed.

She seemed to have acquired a serenity with her new life that made her that much more dramatic.

"There's one more tray," Karma replied. "Is that it?"

Jo handed Karma a hot pot, took the empty tray from her, then handed her the other pot. "I've got more in the back room. Do we need more champagne?"

Amy looked under the white table skirt and saw a single bottle of champagne in a tub of ice. "Yes," she replied.

"There's a small fridge in the basement. I stashed a couple of bottles in there. I'll send Ryan down for it if I can find him." She looked around at the sea of bodies.

Amy poured champagne for another taker. "I'll go for it as soon as I can get away. Is Nancy selling lots of books?"

Jo smiled widely. "Last I heard, she was over one hundred. And it doesn't hit the stands till tomorrow." She pointed to the very happy shop owner hovering at Nancy's shoulder and chatting with a buyer while Nancy signed her book.

Nancy looked stunning in a red silk jacket over a black shirt and pants. Her dark hair was caught back in an elegant knot.

"All right." Karma set the pots down at the end of

the table and handed Jo an empty one. "Maybe Heron Point will put her on the bestseller list all by itself."

Jo nodded. "Well, she better remember her friends when she buys a vacation home in Cozumel. I'll get more cookies and be right back."

"I wish we had thought to bring ourselves a tip jar," Karma said with a grin as everyone refilled on goodies and champagne. "We could be making a bundle."

Amy laughed and continued to fill glasses, very much aware of how little of the bubbly was left in the basin filled with ice.

She looked up during a lull to see Jave, Nate, Ryan and Tom collected in a group at Nancy's table. All elegantly groomed and wearing suits, they snagged her attention and held it. Even *GQ* magazine, she thought, would have been hard put to find a more handsome collection of men.

Jave and Nate seemed to have shed the nervous energy their work as doctors required, and appeared relaxed and lighthearted. Nate had apparently teased Nancy with some remark that made Jave give him a punitive but friendly shove.

Ryan had none of the dignified banker about him tonight, but seemed to be in a party mood. When Jo sidled by him, empty tray in hand, he caught her wrist and kissed her lightly. He asked her something to which she responded with a shake of her head and another kiss. Then she headed for the back room.

But Tom was something else. She found it astonishing that a man whom she'd always thought had the slim-hipped, thick-shouldered body made for the jeans and flannel shirts he always wore could look so heart-stoppingly handsome in the more constricting shirt and tie and pin-striped suit. He had a hand in one pants pocket, and a brightly wrapped gift in the other.

Amy watched him give it to Nancy. Jave sat on the edge of the table as she unwrapped it, and Nate, Ryan and Pam, the shop owner, closed in to see what it was.

Nancy held up a pen whose beautifully faceted silver barrel glittered in the overhead light. She stood and came around the desk to hug Tom.

Jave, Amy thought, looked pleased. She knew how much he loved his family, and she could only guess how satisfying it was to find that the woman he loved, loved his family as well.

Amy was momentarily lost in fantasies of what it would be like to feel that kind of bond within one's family. She loved hers and she knew they cared about her, but she was just too different from her parents and her sisters to be able to relate to them—or them to her. While love was a comfort, it didn't completely replace the unity created by people who simply understood one another.

Amy turned at the request of a party-goer for more champagne, then looked up to see Steve Fuller talking to Diantha and trying to sidle away from her toward the refreshment table.

Amy decided it was a good time to retrieve the champagne in the basement. She warned Karma that she would be gone for a few minutes, then pulled off the tea towel that covered her vanilla silk shirt and beige skirt. She wound her way through the guests gathered in little knots of conversation, books tucked under their arms, and opened the basement door.

She flipped on the light over the stairs and made her way down carefully, aware of a sense of awkwardness in her seldom-worn black leather pumps. But once she reached the bottom, she couldn't find another light switch. The light over the stairs lit the forward half of the room, but since she saw no refrigerator there, she presumed it was located somewhere in the dark half under the stairs.

Ignoring all the old childhood stories of creatures that lived in dark and musty basements, she went carefully into the shadows.

She touched spinner racks of books, tripped over old displays, kicked aside a cardboard dump that had fallen over. She paused to peer into the dark but found nothing. Then she turned to her right, aware suddenly of a spine-chilling sense of being watched, and saw a pair of blue eyes under the stairs catch the light from above.

Her heart rocketed against her side and she screamed. Limbs light with the sudden rush of adrenaline, she spun around to run and found a pair of dark eyes looking down on her.

She screamed again and swung out, terror now a galvanizing force within her.

"Whoa, whoa!" a familiar voice said as a pair of hands, also familiar, caught her wrists. "It's me. What are you doing?"

"Tom!" Amy caught his arm and pointed to the stairs. "There! Someone's there!"

She felt the tension in him, but he remained still for a moment, then when there was not a sound or a movement, he reached to the back of a support beam under the stairs and the dark half of the basement was filled with light.

Amy peered around Tom's shoulder and saw the blue eyes. Then realized with a groan of self-deprecation that they were glass eyes—in a molded plastic face that belonged to the animated Santa that graced the shop's window at Christmastime.

She saw Tom struggle to withhold a laugh. "If I kill him for you," he said in a voice strained with suppressed amusement, "it could endanger your Christmas wish list."

She punched his shoulder and went to the refrigerator now clearly visible in the far corner. "Very funny. How come *you* know where the light switch is?"

"Easy," he replied, coming to stand behind the open refrigerator door. "I installed it when I built some shelves for Pam."

"Well, you couldn't have hidden it better if you'd tried."

"Pam knows where it is, and she's usually the only one who comes down here."

Amy removed two bottles of champagne from the rack on the bottom and held them out to Tom. "Would you take these upstairs for me, please?"

"Sure." He took them from her by the necks and rested them on the top of the door.

"You don't have to wait for me," she said, wishing he would go. She bent to reach two more bottles, feeling as though the musty basement had sapped all her energy and her air. It was difficult to breathe, to think. "Go on. Karma's waiting for those."

"I'll wait for you," he insisted with a grin. "Just in case Santa comes to life and decides you belong on the naughty list."

She rose with the bottles and closed the refrigerator door with her hip. She made a scornful sound. "Ha. As though you'd come to my defense."

She tried to walk around him, but he stepped into her

path. His eyes were clearly puzzled. "You think I wouldn't?"

He would come to her defense in any physical danger; she was sure of that. But when she'd needed him emotionally, he ran. And she hated that she still reacted to him this way, pulse racing, breathing shallow, heart yearning.

"I think you wouldn't," she replied, and tried again to move past him.

Again, he sidestepped. "Why?"

"Because," she said quietly, looking him straight in the eye, "you're afraid of me."

She got as far as the stairs before Tom caught her and turned her around. He had put the champagne bottles somewhere between the refrigerator and the stairs, and his hands were closed around her upper arms like manacles.

Tom didn't know a man in town who would react with any patience to the suggestion that he was afraid of a woman—nineties' political correctness notwithstanding. But more than that, he knew what this particular woman meant by it, and he was getting tired of the issue.

"*Afraid* of you?" he asked flatly.

"Why else would you have run off just when we were becoming intimate?" she retorted, her stubborn jaw set, her hands white-knuckled as she continued to hold the bottles of champagne trapped against his chest. She was tired of the issue, too. "When you finally *knew* you could absolve yourself of even a suggestion of blame in Davey's death? Why?"

He tightened his grip on her and gave her a shake. "If you'd listened to me instead of slamming the door on me when I came over to explain it to you," he said, his temper just under control, "you'd have the answer to that, wouldn't you?"

"Oh, I have it," she said with that frosty tilt of her chin that always made him long for a tub of icy water to dump her into. "You're afraid of me. You think if I become important to you, you might be happy. And if you're happy, you'll have to get on with your life, and you're afraid that you can't. You're no longer the story-book hero in the fireman's hat running to the rescue of a screaming woman. You're just a guy with a scarred leg that still causes him a lot of pain, with memories that still give him nightmares, and with a heart that's just a little empty without sirens and firetrucks, and the call of the flames. And deep down, you think it's over. And maybe you want it to be."

He had to punish her for that. She couldn't fill his brain and his dreams, then stake him out over the coals of his past and poke him with a stick.

He took the bottles from her, set them on the stairs, then yanked her back when she tried to escape him. "*You're* the one who's scared," he said. "You're the one who can't love and trust without knowing every thought in my head, without understanding every little corner of my soul. You can't just want me, you have to *own* me. Well, that isn't love, that's slavery."

Her face paled with anger. "Then consider yourself emancipated," she said, and tried to pull away again.

He held firm. "You can't free me," he said angrily, "because you never did own me. That's what you're afraid of. That you never will."

"I do *not*," she shouted at him, "want to own you. I just wanted to be allowed close enough to try to figure out what the hell was going on with you."

"All right," he said, drawing a breath to calm himself, "you want to read me? You want to prove you're not afraid? You want proof that I'm not?"

He dropped his hands from her, and she knew what he intended instantly. She was free to go, but she would prove her claim—she would understand his—only if she stayed.

He rested his hands on his hips and challenged her with a look, his anger slipping into something even more elemental, more dangerous—masculine arrogance.

"Make me believe you could care about me," he dared her, "without having me under lock and key."

Amy looked into his unrelenting stare with the thought that hurrying back upstairs would be the wiser course of action. But she'd taken up child care as a profession; obviously she hadn't a clue about wisdom.

And this was something she was not going to be able to go around in her life. It was going to keep getting in her way. She had to deal with Tom Nicholas. She had to show him.

Unsure if she was being brave or reckless, she slipped her arms inside his open coat and around him and put her hands to his back, just above his belt. She tried to use them to pull him toward her, but he remained firmly planted. Part of his independence manifesto, she guessed. She had to go to him.

So she did. She came right up against him, breast to chest, thigh to thigh, and everything in between in direct contact, except for the cotton-and-wool blend of her skirt and his slacks.

She saw the flare of reaction in his eyes, felt the guarded alertness in him as he maintained his hands-on-hips position.

"The question," she asked very quietly, "is does a woman want to put all this effort into a man who will not only keep his heart locked away from her, but his body, too? Even a very determined woman works best with a little response.''

''A man responds best,'' he said, still not moving, ''to a woman who isn't trying to change him.''

Amy remembered their days together so clearly, and the abject misery she felt when he held her in his arms and still managed to exclude her from what he thought and felt.

''I never wanted to change you,'' she said with all the sincerity with which she had once loved him. ''I just wanted to *know* you.''

His eyes darkened, and he dropped his hands, distracted, it seemed, by something he saw in her face.

She took advantage of his vulnerability, and with the added height her heels afforded her, she stretched up just a little and claimed his mouth.

He did not resist. In fact, she congratulated herself on her consummate skill, as he seemed to become pliable in her arms. He leaned down to accommodate her, his arms came lightly around her, and he responded to her searching kiss with surprising cooperation.

He parted his lips when her tongue probed for access, then he parried with it as she explored. He held her kiss as her hands wandered into his hair, teased his ear, then went back inside his jacket to rove his back.

She finally drew away, nipping his chin for good measure. His expression was unreadable but his body wasn't. He'd liked that. She'd been close enough to know. She thought she deserved to gloat a little.

''So,'' she said breathlessly, with a superior glance at him, ''I guess we've proved that I'm not afraid.''

He seemed to take exception to the look in her eye; his own expression darkened further.

Now, she thought, was a good time to leave. She turned to pick up the bottles, but he caught her arm and pulled her back to him, his eyes filled with purpose.

"Now," he said, "it's my turn to prove a thing or two."

Oh, no. They'd already pushed the limits of conduct at a business party. She looked at him warily and he raised a questioning eyebrow. "Or is the issue of your courage in question again?"

Before she could answer, he combed the fingers of one hand into her hair, used them to tip her mouth up to him, and claimed it with all the proprietary conviction of a lover.

All the gentleness with which he'd responded to her kiss was gone, and in its place was a ruthless command of everything his lips and hands touched—and both seemed to be everywhere.

His lips roved her face—her eyes, her earlobes, her mouth, her throat—as his hands swept all the way from her shoulder blades to her hips and remained there to hold her to him as he kissed her so deeply she felt her heart leap up in response, as though trying to reach him.

It felt as though fire roared through her, flushing her cheeks, stinging her eyes, heating every part of her in contact with any part of him.

He raised his head, and she felt as though she were made of rags, as though she might flop to the floor if he let her go.

The door at the top of the stairs opened, and Jo's voice shouted, "Amy? Are you down there?"

She had to draw a breath to find her voice. "Yes," she replied, hidden from view by a turn in the stairs. "It took me a few minutes to find the fridge. I'll be right up."

"Okay. Steve Fuller's looking for you."

Amy caught Tom's eye and saw amusement there. "Tell him I'll be right up," she said, pulling out of Tom's arms.

The door closed. Amy picked up the bottles off the stairs as Tom went to retrieve his.

"So, neither of us is afraid," she said, her emotions in turmoil, her heart beating too rapidly for her to think clearly. "You're emancipated, and I'm a business-woman now with new priorities. We should be able to function like two reasonable people."

She started up the steps, but he stopped her again, the two bottles caught in his left hand. She looked down into his even stare. He came up two steps until they occupied the same one. "If we're to 'function like two reasonable people,'" he said quietly, giving added emphasis to her words, "you have to get straight on the notion that you've freed me."

She nodded quickly, wanting nothing more at the moment than to get out of this damned basement. "Poor choice of words. I apologize. You're not emancipated because I never owned you. I forgot. I just meant you were..." Now she'd talked herself into a corner and didn't know where to go with her explanation. Mostly, because she didn't understand their status herself. "You know...that I have no hold on you."

He stunned her when he shifted his weight and admitted gravely, "Actually, you do. What I meant was that *you* can't free me from what I feel for you. I feel it just because I do, because I want to."

While Amy stared at him open-mouthed, trying to decide how to react to that admission, he loped up the stairs and disappeared into the buzzing crowd.

Amy managed to avoid Steve Fuller until the party

wound down and nearly everyone had left except Jave, Nancy and Tom. Nate and Karma helped Jo and Ryan clear away and clean up while Amy turned the serving table over to fold the legs. She became suddenly aware of Diantha's absence.

"Where's Diantha?" she asked the group. But a guffaw of laughter erupted among the men over something Nate had said, and no one heard her.

"She left early, complaining of a headache." Steve Fuller appeared to help her with the table. "I told her not to worry about you, that I'd take you home. I tried to find you to tell you, but Mrs. Foster said you were in the basement."

"Ah." She nodded, aware of Tom turning in their direction. She smiled brightly at Steve. "Thank you," she said. "I'd appreciate that."

Everyone left together, the store manager waving them off and thanking them for the liveliest evening she'd had in years.

They stood in a large group on the sidewalk in the fragrant early fall darkness. Nancy hugged Jo, Karma and Amy for all their efforts with the food, then hugged the men just because, she said, "There hasn't been a kinder or more handsome foursome of heroes since the Three Musketeers and d'Artagnan."

"Well!" Nate exclaimed. "That must mean we get to go wenching."

"No," Karma corrected him clearly, "it doesn't." She grabbed his arm and pulled him toward their car.

He waved a laughing good-night.

"Who needs him, anyway," Ryan said to Jave and Tom, and the three turned, as though prepared to go wenching on their own.

Jo caught Ryan.

"Aw, come on," Ryan grumbled. "I was just going to watch."

Jo hooked an arm around his waist and smiled into his eyes. "If you come home with me, you can actually participate."

"Ooh," he said, obviously lured away by the promise. He waved to his friends. "You'll have to carry on without me." And they turned in the direction of the side street.

Jave looked at Tom. "I guess it's just you and me."

Nancy smiled at Jave sweetly. "Guess what? It's just him. 'Night, Tom."

Jave shrugged helplessly as Nancy led him away.

Tom turned to Amy and Steve. "I don't suppose," he said to Steve, "that the high school principal could be caught wenching?"

Steve laughed. "Another time, maybe. Tonight I promised to take Amy home."

Tom nodded amiably, apparently unaffected by that news. After her experience with him in the basement, Amy couldn't help a certain annoyance.

It mounted when Tom smiled at her and said with a significance in his eyes only she would have interpreted, "Let me know about the leaded-glass window tomorrow, will you?" His expression was bland, but there was an I-told-you-so in his eyes.

Fifteen minutes later, Amy stood on her front porch in Steve Fuller's embrace, being kissed with tender care.

She looped her arms around his neck, wanting to give the experience a real chance, wanting to see, if she put her heart into it, if there could be something here.

His lips were tender but impassioned, his touch was gentle but competent. It was nice. It was really nice. But her heart didn't seem to be interested.

She guessed when he drew away that he'd read her reaction. His smile was wry and regretful.

"How long have you been in love with Nicholas?" he asked.

"Nicholas," she said, deliberately misunderstanding, "is married to one of my best friends."

He scolded her with a look. "You know which Nicholas I mean. I was told you two had broken up a couple of years ago."

She leaned back against her front door, her smile apologetic. "We did. It's over. I just...have too much on my mind for romance."

"Really." He braced a hand against the door and looked down at her doubtfully. "That must be why the two of you came up from the basement looking like you'd been necking in some hayloft."

Hayloft. Funny he should say that. She remembered sitting in her hayloft with Tom and feeling as though her entire life had just been dropped out a window, like a bale of hay.

"We'd been arguing," she said, rummaging in her purse for her key.

"Arguing doesn't put that look in your eye," he disputed quietly. "And he looks at me with direct hostility."

Amy took exception to that. "He's always been very polite to you."

He dropped his hand and put both in his pockets. "Yes, he has, but I get the feeling if I touched you in his presence, he'd rip my throat out."

Amy frowned. "Well, that's a lovely image to go to sleep on. Thanks for the ride home."

"Look." He stopped her before she could push the door open and smiled thinly in the dim porch light. "I wanted to know if there could be anything between us, and I got my answer." His smile widened slightly. "There is something between us. It's Tom Nicholas." He leaned down and kissed her cheek. "If you ever do decide it really is over between you, call me. Good night, Amy."

"Good night."

Amy waved as he drove away, then pushed her way into the empty house. It was shadowy and quiet, and she absorbed the stillness, knowing that in less than eight hours it would be chaos in this room.

She sank onto the sofa and put a hand to her heart, feeling chaos there, too. And Tom Nicholas was going to be working in her backyard for the next two months. Great. By the time the barn was ready for Kids & Co.'s expansion, she should be ready for an asylum.

Chapter Seven

GARRETT: Don't look at me. I didn't do it. I didn't even see it. I went into the bathroom to be by myself, then Kate followed me in and misinterpreted my intentions and stayed to help me do what I didn't really want to do in the first place. Anyway, what do you expect? You know how girls are. Chelsea and Malia must have ripped into it when our backs were turned. You should tell that kid to learn to put her things away.

MALIA: I helped, but it was Chelsea's idea. She's lusted after it ever since Darcy started bringing it. And, you know, considering she left it on the floor, you can't blame us for thinking she was through with it.

CHELSEA: Okay, it was me. But Beautiful Brenda couldn't breathe in that box! It was probably like being in jail. And then she got all these cool new clothes and she couldn't even put them on! Mom says we have to shake off the things that hold us back—and I think that includes the plastic wrapper from the store.

"Oh, no!"
Amy stood in the kitchen with Rodney, trying to

freeze a wad of gum out of his hair with an ice cube, and heard Kate's plaintive cry. Even considering Kate's tendency to drama, the sound sent a finger of dread along Amy's spine.

"What is it?" she shouted, still applying the cube to the gum.

There was a moment's hesitation. Amy felt a second finger of dread.

"You'd better come," Kate said in a weak voice Amy didn't like at all.

She sat Rodney in a kitchen chair and handed him the Baggie-wrapped ice cube. "Hold that to the gum, sweetie," she said, and hurried into the living room where the sight that met her eyes drew a heartfelt groan from deep inside her.

Three of the world's most beautiful toddlers sat in a circle surrounded by the most advanced educational toys and the most practical tried-and-true playthings money could buy—and what they'd chosen to play with was Darcy's "investment."

The plastic wrap had been efficiently ripped off of both the doll and the clothes. Tiny garments were strewn everywhere, the bridal veil had been ripped off Brenda's head, and her hair looked as though she'd seen *Alien* one too many times.

Chelsea held Brenda in her scrap of blankie and did not look willing to relinquish her.

Amy closed her eyes and wondered why she hadn't gone into something more simple—like the diplomatic corps in the Middle East.

"I'm sorry," Kate said, sounding close to tears. "Garrett went into the bathroom and sat on the potty chair, only he was still wearing everything, so I went to help him. The girls were playing nicely with the beads, and I hadn't noticed that Darcy left her Brenda when she and Truman and the Nicholas boys went outside to play.'' Kate ended with a sigh. ''She's going to be so upset. I think it's a transference thing for her, you know. Oh, it's all my fault!''

Amy put an arm around Kate's shoulders, trying desperately to think of a solution. ''It's all right. Who'd have ever thought Darcy would leave it behind?''

''This will ruin the whole afternoon for her,'' Kate said, wringing her hands. ''The pumpkin patch won't be any fun for her when she sees what's happened to Brenda.''

''Okay.'' Amy went into action. She scooped Chelsea into her arms and pointed to the rubble on the floor. ''If we can get it all picked up, maybe she won't notice Brenda's missing until after we go to the pumpkin patch. Rodney!''

The boy came out of the kitchen holding the ice cube to his head. Then he spotted the bad-hair-day Brenda in Chelsea's arms and the clothes strewn all over the floor, and said feelingly, ''Holy s—-!''

''Rodney!'' Amy scolded.

''I mean, darn!'' he said apologetically. ''But Darcy's going to kick a— I mean, butt, when she gets back!''

''We're not going to say anything to her about it until after we've been to the pumpkin patch,'' Amy said firmly. ''Understand?''

He got down on his knees beside Kate and hurriedly gathered up clothes. He stopped to look up at her. ''You mean we're going to lie?''

''No,'' Amy replied. ''I mean, we're going to keep it to ourselves so that she can have fun this afternoon.''

''What if she sees it's missing and tries to find it?''

"We'll hope she'll be too preoccupied with picking out pumpkins to notice."

He looked doubtful but helped Kate pick up the doll clothes, then looked for a second minuscule little shoe.

Amy took Chelsea into the nap room and tried to negotiate for the Brenda doll.

"I'm sorry, Chelsea," she said reasonably. "I know you want to play with it, but it isn't yours. You have to give it back." Amy took hold of Brenda and pulled.

Chelsea shrieked. "No! Mine! No!"

You listen to me, Amy Brown. Brenda has been suffocating in that box for weeks, and I couldn't stand it another moment. We're all mothers in this world, and the children are everybody's children. You wouldn't keep me in a box wrapped in plastic, would you? Well, I saw an injustice and I rectified it. Now she's mine!

"Chelsea, she isn't yours," Amy said patiently. "She belongs to Darcy. Some toys we can share, and others belong to the children who bring them." Amy pulled again.

Chelsea bellowed. "No! Chessy's! No!"

Don't preach to me about ownership! I've had my blankie stolen and flushed, my apple juice ripped off, and my binkie grabbed, and nobody made a fuss about that. Well, you did bring Lia's Uncle Tom to get my blankie, and I appreciate that. But if Darcy wants her Brenda back, tell her to have her mother hire one of the lawyers she works for and see if they don't consider Darcy an abusive parent!

Amy pulled the sturdy little fingers from around Brenda's throat and removed the doll. Chelsea screeched.

"I'm sorry, Chelsea," she said, hiding the doll in a dresser drawer and bouncing Chelsea in her arms to comfort her. "I know that was rotten, but Brenda isn't yours. Come on. We'll find something else for you to play with."

Don't think you're going to buy my silence with a handful of Cheerios or a Cabbage Patch doll. I want Brenda! And I'm going to make your life miserable until I get her! Put that away, I don't want... Mmm. What is it?

Amy probed Chelsea's pursed lips with a spoonful of strawberry ice cream. The toddler stopped screaming and sucked on the spoon, making a face over the cold, then opening her mouth for more.

Hey, what's she got? I want some!

Amy looked down to find Garrett hanging on to her leg, looking soulfully up at the spoon.

If he gets some, I want some!

Malia appeared, reaching up for the spoon. "Lia some!" she cried.

Order had been restored and all signs of Brenda hidden when Darcy and the boys came inside again.

"Okay, everybody get coats on," Amy said before Darcy had a moment to remember that she'd misplaced her "investment." "We're going to Dr. Foster's pumpkin patch."

Darcy, Rodney and Pete hurried to comply. Truman sat in a kitchen chair. Eddy stood beside him, hands in his pockets.

"We're not going," Truman said, pointing to Eddy, then himself. "It's stupid and embarrassing."

Amy handed Chelsea to Kate, who had collected the toddler's coats. The prospect of a trip had the little ones going to the door.

"Why is it stupid?" Amy asked. "You guys don't like the idea of Halloween and trick-or-treating?"

Truman fiddled with one of the rungs on the ladder-back chair, his large, already strong hands moving restlessly. "Yeah, but carving pumpkins is for girls."

"And picking 'em out," Eddy added, "is for babies."

The back door opened and Tom appeared. He opened his mouth to speak, but before he could state his business, Amy said briskly, "Really? Well, Tom's coming."

Tom blinked and started to speak again, but before he could, Truman demanded suspiciously, "He is?" Then, in unison with Eddy, he turned to Tom. "You are?"

Amy sent a plea across the room with her eyes.

"Ah…yeah. I am," Tom said. The look he returned her begged for some clue about what he'd agreed to.

Truman appeared confused. "I thought going to a pumpkin patch was a girlie thing to do."

Amy saw in Tom's eyes that he grasped the issue. He remained in the doorway. His jeans and green-and-white flannel shirt were streaked with old paint and covered with fresh sawdust. She could smell the Douglas fir across the room.

Tom grinned. "Most guys like activities that include girls," he said to the boys. "And there's nothing girlie about a place that invites ghosts, bats and big hairy spiders, is there?"

Truman and Eddy looked at each other and appeared to reconsider.

"I'll dust myself off and change my shirt," Tom told Amy with an expression that suggested he'd expect to be repaid for this, "and be right back."

OVER THE LAST FEW WEEKS, Tom had spent enough time around Amy's house to know that one had to have nerves on a very low setting in order to cope. Children, it seemed, were always going full tilt at high volume.

He was somewhat used to that with his nephews and niece, but eight children, particularly in an excited mode, could deafen a man and make him crazy.

But Amy, who seemed to have difficulty with office jobs, moved among the children with a serenity that astounded him. She was usually carrying one child and had two others clamoring for her attention, with another shouting to her from another room, yet she somehow managed to give everyone the attention required and fill all needs.

And that was how it was at the pumpkin patch. The day was blustery, the afternoon sky threatening rain as they wandered through the large patch Nate and Karma had put in at Amy's urging. Wood smoke curled from the A-frame's chimney, and its pungent perfume filled the air.

Tom had Malia in his arms, and Truman and Eddy flanking him, still a little afraid of appearing less than masculine, as he wandered among the fat orange pumpkins strewn along curly, big-leaved vines.

Karma had come home from her office early to help, and Garrett ran to her when she came out to welcome them. She scooped him up and met Amy, who held on to Chelsea's hand.

Darcy, Pete and Rodney ran freely up and down the rows, stopping to inspect, dismiss, reconsider and wrap their arms around the pumpkins to judge size.

The children's laughter and excitement became infectious, and soon Truman and Eddy had gone off to explore and Tom was left to trail Malia, who had wriggled down and was conducting her own search for the perfect pumpkin.

It was an hour before decisions were made, pumpkins were cut from the vine, and the bottoms marked with the appropriate child's name. Tom and Truman loaded the pumpkins into Amy's van, then Karma served apple juice and doughnuts in her big country kitchen.

Tom decided as he drove back to Amy's with Truman and Eddy beside him, and Rodney and Pete in the jump seat behind him, that he wouldn't have missed the experience for the world. The boys had pleaded to ride with him while Amy and Kate drove back in Amy's van with Darcy, Chelsea and Malia. Garrett had stayed with his mother.

"You know," Truman said, "I didn't see one ghost, one bat or one hairy spider."

"They probably all went into hiding when we arrived," Tom said matter-of-factly. "I don't think any of them like noise."

"I think you tricked us into going," Eddy accused him with a grin as he leaned around Truman.

Tom glanced at him with an answering grin. "Did you have a good time?"

"Yeah."

"Did you feel like a girl when you carried your thirty-seven-pound pumpkin to the van?"

"No."

"Then, why are we talking about it?"

Truman studied him a moment, then said frankly, "You're kind of weird, you know?"

Tom laughed. "So I've been told."

"You hear about Darcy's Brenda doll?" Rodney asked.

"No." Tom glanced at him in the mirror. "What about it?"

"She left the box on the floor when she came out to play with us, and Chelsea ripped it open and messed up the doll's hair. She had the clothes all over the place, and I had to help clean up."

Tom imagined Darcy's distress and couldn't decide if having the doll forcibly removed from its box would have a good or bad effect on her.

"She doesn't know about it yet," Pete contributed. "Amy didn't want to spoil the trip to the pumpkin patch. She's gonna tell her when we get back. Rodney had to promise to be quiet, then we all had to promise, too."

Tom watched the road, thinking about Darcy's effort to keep the gift from her father in the pristine condition in which she'd received it. He remembered that he'd treated his life that way, that his strengths and his talents had been like a gift, tightly wrapped, contained. Then the fire had ripped off the wrapping and spilled out the contents and just like everything removed from its original package, things hadn't fit back in in the same way.

There were things that had to be folded to be put back in, things that hung out, things that didn't fit in at all.

"I mean, it's stupid when you think about it," Truman said. "Carrying around a doll in a box. But she liked it that way. Things never stay the way you like them."

Tom considered that an astute observation from the boy who'd lost his mother.

Rodney sighed. "It was from her dad and she never gets to see him. That's why she did it."

Eddy made a sympathetic face. "She's pretty dorky sometimes, but I feel sorry for her."

Pete sighed from the jump seat. "Me and Eddy used to feel real bad when our mom left. You know, the other mom. Before Nancy."

Tom nodded, commiserating, and thinking that it was scary how perceptive these children were, but warming to see their genuine concern.

He got to the intersection, watched Amy make the left turn toward her home, and hesitated. He turned to his companions. "Guys," he said. "I have a plan."

AMY WASHED THE PUMPKINS outside with the hose while Kate and Darcy kept the toddlers from getting involved. Then they carried the pumpkins into the kitchen, and Darcy disappeared into the living room.

Kate caught Amy's eye in distress. "I should be the one to tell her," Kate said quietly. "It's my fault."

"It's nobody's fault," Amy insisted. "You keep the babies busy and I'll tell her."

She'd just spoken the words when Darcy came running back into the kitchen, eyes round and distressed. "Amy?" she asked. "Have you seen Brenda? I didn't take her to the pumpkin patch, but I can't find her."

"I know where she is," Amy said.

Darcy sighed with relief, then asked, "Where? Where is she?"

Amy led Darcy to the nap room where she'd stashed the doll among the crib linens. She sat her on one of two single beds and sat beside her.

"I think you must have left her on the floor when you and the boys went outside to play," Amy said calmly. "I'm afraid...she got out of the box."

Darcy's eyes widened and then filled instantly with tears. "Truman did it!"

"No. He was outside with you, remember? I didn't see what happened until Brenda was already out of the box, but I think it was Chelsea. You know she didn't do it on purpose. She's too little to know she was doing something wrong." Amy forced a cheerful smile. "But I think Brenda's fine." She opened the drawer and handed the doll with her rumpled hair to Darcy. "I'm sure if we comb her hair and put her veil back on, she'll be okay."

Darcy took the doll from Amy and stared at her in horror. Then she watched with the same expression as Amy spread the clothes out on the bed.

"When I was a little girl," Amy said, desperate to erase the anguish from Darcy's face, "Brenda came with a wardrobe trunk for keeping her clothes in. I think my mom still has it in the attic where I used to live. I'll ask her to look for it, and we can put all Brenda's cl—"

Darcy's tears began to fall, and she ran a hand over the rumpled hair. "It was a investment!" she said plaintively. She began to sob and held the doll to her. "My dad sent it!"

Amy held her and rocked her, at a complete loss over what to do for her. It was an offense against nature to expect a child to keep a toy in a box, but she imagined that Darcy had somehow confused the love she felt for the father she never saw with the gift he'd sent her, and wanted it forever protected in its wrapper. And it was also a way to help the mother she loved as well—or so her grandmother had made her believe.

"I think your dad would like it if you played with

it,'' Amy said. ''Your mom says she doesn't want you to save it and sell it. She *wants* you to play with it.''

''But she needs the money!''

''Honey, it'll be years before the doll is worth enough to sell it. By then, you'll probably have a job and you can help your mom that way.''

''I wanted her in the box,'' she sobbed, while hugging the doll to her with a fervor that belied her words.

Amy had known that logic would be wasted on the child who had taken the complicated elements of her life and come to an understanding that worked for her, but she'd had to try.

''Well, we've still got the box.'' She pulled that, too, out of the drawer. ''Do you want to see if we can get it all back inside and put plastic wrap over it? Collectibles in their original wrapping are worth more, but you can still get money for them even if they're not. Brenda will still be protected.''

Darcy held the doll away from her, looked into her face and made the hard decision. ''Okay,'' she said.

The babies were holding their pumpkins and watching cartoons when Amy and Darcy came out of the nap room. Kate was picking up toys.

Amy frowned at her. ''Where are Tom and the boys?''

''Tom just called,'' Kate replied, arms filled with colorful plastic. ''He said they took a detour. They'll be back in half an hour.''

''Where did they go?''

Kate shrugged. ''He didn't say.''

Oh, good, Amy thought. Parents would be arriving in twenty minutes and she would have to explain that she didn't know where their children were, except that she'd let them drive off with the carpenter. Yes. That would be a fitting end to a trying day—and possibly her career.

"THERE'S MY DAD'S JEEP," Rodney said as Tom passed it and pulled into Amy's driveway.

Truman pointed to the silver Buick Regal in front of Jave's new white Volvo. "There's my dad's car, too."

"Okay." Tom backed out again and parked on the street. "We'd better leave them room to get out. Climb out on the sidewalk side, and don't dawdle, okay? Your dads are probably anxious to get you home."

The parents appeared less impatient than Tom expected when he followed the four boys into the house. Fuller sat on the sofa in conversation with Jo, who still wore her coat and had dressed Chelsea for outdoors.

Jave and Boomer were dutifully admiring Malia's pumpkin.

Amy stood in a corner with Mrs. Billings, who held a weeping Darcy in her arms. Amy looked across the room and flayed Tom with her eyes.

He groaned silently.

Truman, carrying the package, turned to make sure his friends were following. They stacked up behind him like a row of dominoes. Assured of their support, he led the way to Darcy and thrust the gift-wrapped box at her as though it were a weapon.

She sniffed and looked at it suspiciously, then at the boys.

Mrs. Billings smiled at Truman. "What's this?" she asked. When Truman stammered awkwardly, she looked to Amy for an explanation.

Amy spread her hands helplessly, the anger in her expression turning to confusion as she glanced at Tom.

"It's a present," Eddy said. "Open it, Darcy."

Darcy took the gift, carefully untaped the ends, then the back. As the paper fell away, she held up the Blue Grass Brenda. It had taken twenty minutes for four boys to agree on it when they couldn't find the ill-fated Beautiful Bride Brenda.

"You can save this one," Truman said, "and play with the one your dad sent."

"An' it's only three months older than the other one," Eddy reasoned, "so it should be worth almost as much when you're ready to sell it."

"The lady in the store looked it up," Rodney said, "and it's very collectible."

"And the horse," Pete added with sincere interest, "is really cool!"

It was difficult to tell if Darcy was more shocked by the gift, or by the gesture from the boys who usually loved to persecute her.

"You boys bought this yourselves?" Mrs. Billings asked.

"Well..." Truman pointed behind him to Tom. "We kicked in what we had, but Tom lent us the rest. And he drove us to the toy store. We...you know..." He shuffled nervously, looked to his friends for support, but they all looked the other way. "We knew," he finally finished on his own, "she'd feel bad about Brenda coming out of the box."

The woman looked about to burst into tears. Amy put an arm around her and she pulled herself together. "Well, that's about the nicest present Darcy's ever gotten," she said, hugging each boy in turn. "And it makes me very happy to know she has such good friends."

Darcy sniffed again, handed her mother the box and disappeared into the kitchen. She came back with the

Brenda she'd carried around for months, only now she was out of her box and clutched in her arms.

"Don't forget her clothes," Amy said, retrieving a plastic grocery bag from the kitchen table. She handed it to Darcy's mother and walked her and Darcy to the door.

Ginger Billings turned and cast an embarrassed but smiling glance around the room. "Thank you all for your concern."

Jo stood, holding Chelsea by the hand. "I apologize again for my little vandal."

Ginger shook her head. "It's all right. Goodbye."

She called to Tom, who'd had about enough of the intimacy of the moment and was trying to slip out to the barn.

He stopped at the foot of the steps.

She walked down to him, Darcy behind her and Amy beside her. "You're the carpenter," she said.

"Right." He offered his hand. "Tom Nicholas."

She took it in a warm grip. "You made the pencil holder Darcy came home with the other day."

He tried to ward off gratitude. "A leftover block of four-by-four and a dozen passes with the drill."

She smiled. "But driving the boys to town and lending them the money to buy the doll was more than that. Thank you."

"They wanted to do something for her. I was just the wheels. Darcy's a great kid."

"I've always thought so. Thank you again."

"My pleasure."

Tom stood with Amy to wave off the Billingses, then finally made his escape.

Or so he thought. He looked up from hanging Sheetrock on the loft wall and found Jave standing behind him.

"What do I owe you?" Jave asked.

Tom picked up a couple of nails from the sawhorse table at his side. "A little peace and quiet, respect, probably half a dozen apologies for various..."

"I mean," Jave interrupted, "for the boys' share of the doll."

"Nothing." Tom turned away from him to hammer in a nail. "It's a deal between me and the boys. They're going to help me with a couple of projects."

"You really think you're going to get work out of them?"

Tom turned back to him. "Sure. They promised. If you have any more questions, you'll have to save them because Amy's paying me by the hour, and it just cost her sixty bucks to take me to a pumpkin patch to convince the boys that it wasn't sissy stuff."

Jave grinned. It was that "I know you better than you know yourself" grin that always annoyed Tom. "And then you took it upon yourself to show them that kindness isn't for sissies, either."

"They wanted to do something for Darcy," Tom insisted. "I happened to have the Visa card. Now, get out of here before I'm forced to drywall right over you."

Jave didn't seem to feel threatened. "Thank you," he said. "It was good for them to see concern and compassion for someone else in someone they admire."

Tom put an arm around his shoulders, a score of warm and heartfelt responses on the tip of his tongue. But those things were hard for him. And he knew Jave knew it. So he walked him to the new stairs. "You're welcome," he said. "And I'm sure it would be good for them to see punctuality in you. So take them home before they miss dinner. Give my love to Nancy.''

Jave spared him further discomfort with a knowing nod. "See you at Diantha's on Halloween."

"Right." Tom groaned. "Costumes."

Jave ran lightly down the steps. "Yes," he called back. "And you can't come as a carpenter."

Boomer walked into the barn as Jave left, Fuller right behind him.

Boomer had his wallet in hand. "We want to pay you for the…"

"No," Tom said, coming the rest of the way down the stairs. "It was a deal between the boys and me. They're going to work it off."

Fuller raised an eyebrow. "Truman?"

Boomer shook his head fatalistically. "Rodney's going to owe it all back to you in cuss fines."

Tom laughed and pushed away the bill Fuller tried to hand him. "Thanks, but the boys wanted to do it. They borrowed the money from me, and they should pay it back to me themselves, don't you think?"

Boomer studied him a moment, then pocketed his wallet. Fuller stuffed the bill back in his pocket.

"Well, hell. Thank you." Boomer reached a hand toward him.

Tom shook it. "You're welcome. Rodney's a nice kid."

Fuller took his hand, his expression half gratitude, half resentment. He was close to making that move on Amy, Tom guessed.

"Truman talks about you all the time," he said. "He's gone from wanting to be a rodeo rider to wanting to be a carpenter."

Tom nodded. "Good choice. Sawhorses are a lot easier to ride."

Fuller measured him with a steady look, then gave him a reluctant smile. "Thanks. I like knowing other people care about him."

All right, Tom thought. So he wasn't so bad.

The men left, and Tom was halfway up the stairs again when a feminine voice called his name. He turned to find Jo, a checkbook in her hand, delving into her purse, apparently for a pen.

"God!" Tom exclaimed, going down again to meet her. "What is wrong with everyone? It was a measly thirty bucks for a doll. That's all! It was a deal between the boys and me and we're going to square up."

Jo treated him to the smile that made her coffee bar the most popular watering hole in three counties. "But my daughter was responsible for…"

"The way I heard it, no one saw who did it. Chelsea just happened to be holding the evidence when it was discovered. I've seen both Malia and Garrett at work. Either of them is clever enough to do it and frame someone else."

She found a pen and looked around to find a place to sit and write the check.

Tom took the pen from her, dropped it into the huge satchel hanging over her shoulder, put an arm around her and walked her across the field. "You're not going to pay me for it. The boys' fathers, my brother included, seem to think it was a good object lesson for the boys, so we're letting the deal stand."

She frowned at him. "It was my understanding they were all coming back here to pay you their shares."

"I talked them out of it," he said.

"But I feel as though I should…"

"No," Tom said firmly. "I'm sure that's a word you've heard before. Ryan must use it on you all the time."

She laughed as they reached the walkway and he ushered her onto it. "He does, he just isn't usually able to make it stick."

Tom nodded, spotting Amy holding Chelsea and standing by Jo's van across the street. "Well, see, that's the difference between bankers and carpenters. Bankers get soft sitting behind a desk, so when their women challenge them, they're forced to back down. But we carpenters are throwing heavy stuff around all the time and building up our pecs and biceps, so that in a crunch, we can say no and mean it."

They stopped on the sidewalk, and she turned to him with a look so femininely superior that he found himself pitying Ryan. "One day, when you're married, and your wife and children have you wound around their little fingers, you'll remember that you said that and laugh at yourself."

"You think so."

"Yes." She reached up to kiss his cheek, then pat it affectionately. "But meanwhile, go ahead and live the fantasy. See you at Diantha's."

"Right." He waved when she reached the other side of the street, then loped back to the barn and thought that he could get the wall done in an hour if he wasn't interrupted again.

He realized that was a vain wish five minutes later when he heard footsteps on his new stairs. He was going to take the damn things down, he thought, as he turned to see who the new intruder was.

It was Amy. He remembered the look she'd given him in the house when he'd returned with the boys, and guessed she was going to chew him out for taking them to town without telling her first.

He dropped his hammer into the toolbox and gave up on the wall. He pulled up a sawhorse and gestured her toward another facing his.

She was carrying a small pumpkin, and she stood holding it in her arms for a minute while she looked around, admiring the two walls that were finished.

"You're almost ready to paint up here!" she said, obviously pleased.

"I could have started in the afternoon, but I've had a lot of disruptions." He wiped his hands on a rag and tossed it into a trash box. Then he gave her his full attention, prepared to accept the reprimand without complaint.

"I have two things for you," she said, holding out the pumpkin. "This is just to remind you that you gave up your time for us—to prove to the boys that you're never too grown-up for fun traditions."

He was touched. The pumpkin was only a four or five pounder, but it was nicely rounded, without a scar, and had apparently been washed by a careful hand. The stem had a curl of vine still attached that made it aesthetically perfect.

"Without your mom there," she said, "there's probably nothing at home to remind you that it's Halloween."

It was hard for him to think of that as a bad thing, because Halloween meant Diantha's party, and that meant a costume. And Jave had just shot down the only idea he had.

She'd said she had two things for him, yet there was nothing else in her hands.

"The second thing," he guessed, "has to be a lecture

about taking off with the kids without telling you where we were going. I'm sorry. I thought we'd be back before the parents arrived.''

''I was embarrassed that I had to tell the parents that I didn't know where you'd taken the boys,'' she admitted. ''But when they heard they were with you, no one seemed to mind particularly. And you did call. But it would be nice if you didn't do that again.''

''I concluded that myself.''

''Good. But that wasn't the second thing.''

''It wasn't?''

''No.'' She stood. ''Please put the pumpkin down.''

All right. Apparently he was going to need his hands free. That sounded promising. He balanced the pumpkin on the sawhorse.

''Stand up.''

He did, thinking this interruption was suddenly taking a very interesting turn.

She put her arms around his neck, pulled his head down and kissed him with a sweetness that hit him too deeply, too emphatically to allow passion to take over. Almost. That is, he knew by the spirit in which she offered the kiss that it shouldn't, so he held it down.

She was slow and sweet and thorough. Then she held him tightly and rested her forehead against his shoulder. ''You and the boys made the whole incident work in Darcy's favor, when it could have just made her so unhappy. And if I'd bought her another doll, or if Jo had replaced it like she wanted to, it wouldn't have been the same. Now she can love the Brenda her father gave her, and save the one from her friends.''

She drew back, and her eyes were brimming with emotion. ''Only the gesture was so sweet, she might have as much trouble keeping that one wrapped up, too.

It's hard not to handle something that's given to you with love. Thank you.''

He had to clear his throat. "You're welcome."

She smiled suddenly, dropped her arms from him and reached into a pocket of her jeans. "I forgot. Actually, I had three things for you." She unfolded the list of supplies and charges he'd given her to look over the day before.

"Something wrong?" he asked.

"Yes." She handed him the list, then started for the stairs. She stopped at the top to look over her shoulder at him and smile. "You have to charge me for the leaded-glass window. You won fair and square. See you in the morning."

Chapter Eight

Things changed at Kids & Co. The difference wasn't enormous, or even dramatic, but Amy saw it and realized that she had to credit Tom for it.

Now when parents dropped off or picked up their children, though they were still in a hurry, they stopped long enough to exchange pleasantries with one another. Darcy and her mother made cookies for the other families as a thank-you for the doll, Boomer arranged for the older children to visit the longshoreman's hall and to watch a ship being loaded with logs.

Jo, insisting on making amends for Chelsea's vandalism, brought a sampler pack of coffees for Ginger Billings, and hot chocolate for Darcy. Ginger raved so much about the coffee to the other parents that regular stops at Coffee Country became a part of everyone's morning routine.

Boomer and Rodney were swearing less.

The children got along the way children always would, bickering continually while learning to coexist. But no one felt excluded anymore. Everyone was part of the fray.

The loft was almost finished. Tom had salvaged a railing with turned balusters from an old office building across the river in Washington, and installed it along the edge of the loft.

Amy wandered into the barn with Truman one night after all the other children were gone. His father had to remain at the school for an open house that night, and Truman was in Amy's care until around ten.

"Do not touch anything," Amy said firmly, seeing Tom's tools strewn around.

"Wow!" Truman knelt to admire the half of the railing that had been stained a warm oak color. The difference in appearance was remarkable. With walls and light, and the leaded-glass window installed where the hay doors were, it looked like an office—but one out of *Architectural Digest.*

"They're still wet," Tom cautioned Truman, then he glanced up from the bucket of stain to smile at Amy. "Hi. What's up?"

His manner hadn't been more than friendly since the night Amy had kissed him, and she wasn't sure what that meant—or what to do about it. Had he lost interest in her, she wondered, or was he waiting for her to make the next move? She couldn't be sure. With the volatility between them, anything more than friendly was chancy on several levels.

So, she'd been coasting, unwilling to risk the wrong move.

"I can't believe how wonderful the window looks," she said, going over to admire it. She turned back to give him a grin over their joke about it.

He caught her eyes but didn't seem to catch the joke. He turned his attention to Truman, who came to stand over his shoulder and watch him work.

Frustrated, Amy walked the length of the loft, pacing

off the distance. Someday, she might be able to afford carpeting.

"Twenty-six feet," Tom said, without looking up from the stain. "And eighteen across."

So he *was* paying attention to her.

"Sam called today from the Secondhand Barn," she said, coming to stand on Tom's other side. "He said he has a few pieces for me to look at that might be right for the office."

"Great." The can of stain was empty. He carried it to a plastic tarp set up across the loft where he had tools and cans of stain. He opened another with the tip of a screwdriver, then picked up a power drill with a stirring attachment on it and the loft was filled with a whirring noise for several seconds while he stirred the stain.

He turned off the drill, removed the attachment and wiped it off with a rag. He drew the last bit of stain out of the old can with his brush.

"You want to come with me?" she asked in a rush, before she could lose her nerve.

This was just what Tom had been waiting for—the smallest sign that there was still feeling for him behind the gratitude. The kiss a week ago had been wonderful, but not something he could react to with anything but friendship.

Of course, she might just want him along on a trip to buy furniture for his professional contribution.

"Sure," he said, trying not to imbue the acceptance with any excitement.

"I know you're expected at Jave's in the afternoon for a costume fitting for the party Thursday," she said. "So I won't keep you very long. I guess Jo commandeered some great stuff from the college's drama department."

Tom was less than enthusiastic about this. He wasn't anxious to see himself in plumes and lace—and even less anxious to appear in public in them.

"I'd rather be worked over with a staple gun," he said.

"It'll be fun," she insisted. "Everybody'll…" She glanced over his shoulder and went suddenly chalk white.

She pushed him aside and ran to the railing. He turned to see Truman holding on to it and walking along the outside of it, dangling over fifteen feet of empty space. Tom's heart leaped to his throat.

By the time he reached them, Amy had caught Truman's arms, but his weight was overbalancing her and she was leaning precariously over rather than drawing the boy back.

Tom caught Amy's upper body in one arm and pulled her back while catching Truman's arm in the other and drawing him toward him. The instant the boy was close enough, Tom reached for him with both hands and lifted him over the railing.

"What is wrong with you?" he barked at the boy.

Amy was between them in an instant, her voice high but quiet. "Tom…" she began.

He pushed her aside. Truman watched him, wide-eyed, his face pale.

Tom felt his heart now rocketing against his ribs and forced himself to calm down. "It's a scientific fact," he said more quietly, "that flesh and bone hitting concrete from a drop of fifteen feet results in sausage. You want to climb around, you do it on the monkey bars, not on my project. You got me?"

Truman swallowed. "Yeah," he said in a small voice.

Amy was giving him that mother-cat look again. "Truman, wait for me downstairs," she said, and waited for the boy to comply. Then she turned to Tom. "Sausage," she said with disapproval. She was still trembling herself, and he watched her put her hands in her jeans pockets, probably in the hope that he wouldn't notice. "That was a charming parable. You think that was the best way to handle that?"

"Last week alone," he said, keeping his voice down, "you found him hanging out your second story window, twelve feet up a Douglas fir on the edge of the woods and hiding in the UPS truck. So far, asking him sweetly not to do things isn't working."

"Intimidation is not a parenting skill!"

"Neither is permissiveness."

She folded her arms belligerently. "You know so much about it, of course, with all the children you have."

He went to pick up the new can of stain. "I've spent a lot of time with Eddy and Pete," he returned calmly, "double trouble in a spray can. There are times when reasoning gets me nowhere. The threat of bodily harm does."

She raised a haughty eyebrow. "You're expecting me to believe that you've actually employed *reason* on something?"

"I don't know if you could believe it," he retorted, "since you probably couldn't even *identify* reason if you found it in your playpen! Now. You're paying me twenty bucks an hour. You really want me to spend it arguing with you?"

She squared her shoulders, bristling. A corner of his mind not completely annoyed with her thought she looked delicious.

"Do you want to keep the job?" she asked.

It was clear the question was a threat. Annoyance became something deeper. "No," he said, "but I have a signed contract that says I have it until I'm finished. I believe it's hysterical-lady proof."

Had the power drill been between her and Tom rather than behind him, Amy would have ventilated him.

As it was, she didn't trust what he might do if she got within reach. So she stalked down the stairs and took Truman back to the house.

TOM PULLED ON HIS WORK jeans and a sweatshirt Saturday morning, thinking he'd take advantage of Amy's absence from home to get some work done. He hadn't seen her after she stormed out on him the night before, and he presumed the invitation to accompany her to Sam's was off.

He grabbed his jacket, opened his front door and discovered he was wrong. He was face-to-face with Amy.

She wore jeans, a denim jacket over a red turtleneck, and a pugnacious expression. Her hand was raised in a fist as though she'd been just about to knock.

"Good morning," she said. The greeting was grudging at best.

"Good morning," he replied in the same tone.

She looked away from him, then back at him, sighed and shifted her weight. "I happen to be a very reasonable woman," she said, as though their conversation of the evening before had not been interrupted by the night. "Except where you're concerned."

He folded his arms, patience strained. He wasn't anxious to fight this out all over again. But she'd made the admission. He should at least listen.

"I've noticed," he said. "What do you suppose accounts for that?"

"It's simple," she answered, her lips quirking as though a smile threatened. "You defy reason."

He rolled his eyes. "That's hardly a quote from the lips of Aristotle."

She laughed outright, hooked an arm in his and drew him down the stairs. "I'm sorry. I guess I was really mad at myself because I hadn't been watching Truman. I know how he is. I just try hard not to yell at the kids. Their mothers don't like that."

Tom had to admit she had a point there. Caring for someone else's children didn't afford you the same options available to you when you reacted to your own.

"I'm sorry, too," he admitted reluctantly. "My adrenaline was pumping. But you should talk to Fuller about him. That kid's got a death wish."

She nodded, her eyes grave with concern. "He's aware of the problem. He thinks part of it is Truman's age, and part of it has to be adjusting to the loss of his mother."

As meddlesome as his own mother was, Tom thought with an unconscious smile, she'd been there every time he'd turned to her throughout his life. He couldn't imagine what it would have been like to have lost her as a boy.

Amy drew a breath suddenly and shook her head. "It's Saturday. I just want to enjoy my freedom. Are you ready?"

He focused on her with a wolfish smile. "To enjoy your freedom?"

She pinched the arm she held. "To come with me to Sam's."

It was easy to put all his annoyance with her aside when she smiled at him with that intimate sweetness.

"Come on." He took her arm and led her to the passenger side of his truck. "We'll take this in case you like the stuff and we have to haul it home."

Amy loved it all. Sam, a burly, bearded man in bib overalls, led them to a back room where he had stashed a turn-of-the-century writing desk with a shallow riser that contained pigeonholes and drawers, and an old barrel-back chair that matched.

Amy sat in the chair and ran a hand over the desk.

"We've got oak filin' cabinets," Sam pointed out, indicating seven or eight four-drawer cabinets across the room, "a credenza and—" he pulled a tarp off something bulky in a corner "—a bookcase."

They made a deal for one of the file cabinets and all the other pieces.

Amy spotted the teapot on their way out. It was a mottled yellow and black with a small, lionlike figure serving as a knob on the lid.

She got down on her knees to inspect it, sitting on a coffee table.

Tom felt himself go weak at her expression. He found the piece ugly, but ran a reverent index finger over the shell-like fluting on the belly of the pot.

Amy knew very little about antiques and dealt mostly in simply used things. But this looked old and special.

"Staffordshire Agateware," Sam said. "About 1760. I checked my books. Lady who brought it in says it went to the colonies with a lady from London. That lady's granddaughter brought it west on a wagon train."

Tom leaned over Amy. "Got a lust for it?" he asked, his voice deep and quiet.

"I was thinking," she replied, "that it would make a great office teapot."

Sam, apparently recognizing vulnerability, moved in with more detail.

"Great-great-great-granddaughter brought it in. She said the lady who brought it west was coming to San Francisco to meet her husband, who was building a hotel. But he was killed when a beam slipped as they were putting it into place. She stayed, though, and used the building for an orphanage."

"Orphanage?" Amy looked up, feeling electricity in her fingertips. "She cared for children," she whispered to Tom.

For an instant they were locked together in the one-in-a-million chance that the pot clearly belonged to her.

Sam smiled over them. "Curious parallel here. She married one of the carpenters working on the building."

Tom looked up at Sam. "We'll take it," he said.

"Wait. How much?" Amy asked practically.

Sam looked apologetic. "It's in perfect condition. The book says..." He named a figure that was beyond Amy's already blown budget. She wanted so much to justify its purchase on the basis of fate, if nothing else, but she'd already spent a lot, and she still had to supply the downstairs of the barn with children's toys and more furniture—the whole point of the renovation.

"We'll take it," Tom repeated.

Amy got to her feet. "I can't," she said firmly. "I've already..."

"You write her up," Tom said to Sam, ignoring her protests, "and I'll start loading the truck. Is Jed here to help me today?"

Sam started toward the counter, tipping his head back and bellowing, "Je-e-ed!"

"Tom, I..." Amy began again.

"Consider it a gift from me," Tom said. "And if you don't like that idea, I'll give you the window back. So it just comes out of your already budgeted expenses."

"But Steve did..." She wanted to be honest without betraying a very nice man. "I mean, I don't know that you could call it a move, exactly, because he was just... I mean, I sort of...encouraged him."

She wasn't sure how she'd wanted Tom to react to that. She just knew it wasn't with a smile and a shrug and the philosophical "It's a free country" with which he did reply.

THEY LOOKED LIKE an illustration from Alexandre Dumas's *The Three Musketeers* come to life in Diantha Pennyman's den. Tom watched his friends, garbed in the Musketeers costumes Jo had borrowed from the college, and shook his head over their affability as they waited for their women, who were helping their hostess refill the buffet table.

It had become tradition to take a brief break at Diantha's annual Halloween party to make plans for the hospital's Christmas party for underprivileged children. Jave usually chaired the event, and all the principals he bullied into helping were present at Diantha's.

Jave talked with Nate and Ryan, his ostrich-plumed hat at a rakish angle, his hand resting negligently on the hilt of a sword, as though he really did know how to use one. His breeches were black and his jacket—or doublet, as Jo had called it—was deep red and trimmed with braid. Around his neck was a deep lace collar, and at his wrist, ruffled cuffs.

His companions were dressed similarly, all wearing

the black breeches and the boots with deep, turned-down cuffs, but Ryan's doublet was dark green, and Nate's gold.

Tom had strongly protested the lavender doublet that had been left for him.

Ryan held a musket at his side, the palm of his hand on the barrel.

Nate held his over his shoulder, as though he'd just returned from hunting quail, or whatever wildlife inhabited the French countryside.

The door burst open and the women finally arrived on a wave of laughter. They were dressed like ladies of the period, in gowns with boned bodices, long skirts and puffed sleeves that became skin-tight below the elbow. They wore the same hairstyle—the back caught up in a bun, the sides hanging in tight ringlets. They looked prim and starched and unlike their free-spirited selves.

Jo carried a tray, which she put down on the coffee table, then distributed paper plates.

The couples helped themselves to snacks, then paired off around the room, Karma in Nate's lap in a big chair, Nancy in a corner of the sofa, Jave on the arm of it beside her, Jo tucked into Ryan's arm at the other end.

Tom, expecting Amy to sit in the middle of the sofa, was surprised when she turned instead and came to join him on a balding brocade love seat by the window.

"Monsieur d'Artagnan," she said with a flirtatious smile. "May I join you?"

"By all means," he replied, returning her smile. "But watch the sword. I think I've been responsible for a few torn skirts this evening."

She widened eyes that were dramatically made up. "I suppose you'll be facing the guillotine."

He leaned toward her. "I don't think it's been invented yet," he said under his voice.

She shrugged as though that made no difference. "Then we'll have to throw you into the Seine."

"But I'm a good swimmer."

"We'll tie weights to your feet."

He studied her with feigned concern. "You're very bloodthirsty, *mademoiselle*."

She fluttered both hands expressively. "I'm French, *monsieur*. It's love or war with us."

"And you've chosen war?"

She rested an elbow on his shoulder and, looking deeply into his eyes said, "Actually, I've chosen love."

It was the sudden silence in the room that alerted them. Tom and Amy turned away from each other to see their friends watching them, the men amused, the women interested.

"I asked," Jave said with exaggerated patience, "if you can make those pencil holder things like you made for the kids. We want to use them for centerpieces at the hospital's Christmas party. Amy thinks they'd not only look good, they could be put to good use when people got them home."

Tom had to force his mind into gear. It wanted to linger on Amy. He gave her a teasing frown. "Thank you, Amy. I needed another project."

She smiled brightly. "The boys can help you to work off their debt."

He closed his eyes in prayer as he considered that prospect. Then he opened them and nodded at Jave. "Sure. I'll do it."

"Good. The girls are on an Old French kick this year, so they're making angels and flowers out of French lace."

"Ah...?" Tom raised his hand.

"Yeah?" Jave asked.

"Pardon me, but how will pencil holders fit into an Old French theme?"

"Easily," Amy replied. "We'll just put the angels and flowers and greenery on florist wire and tuck them into the holes. It'll look great."

Tom looked around the room to see if the idea seemed less than lucid to anyone else. Apparently it didn't.

"Okay," he acceded. "Angels in a pencil holder. That makes sense."

Amy smiled, undaunted. "Everything makes sense at Christmas." Then, to his complete surprise, she leaned toward him and kissed him lightly on the mouth. "Even you, Tom."

Their friends cheered and applauded.

Tom took their ribbing in stride. He'd been hanging back with Amy this week, hoping that giving her space would lighten the tension between them. She'd grumbled at him about the teapot all the way home last Saturday, but he'd noticed on Tuesday that it had a spot of honor in the middle of her hutch.

Tonight she seemed to have taken an aggressive approach to their relationship. It might be time for him to change his battle plan.

Tom's eyes promised payback, and Amy let herself accept that that pleased her. He'd been keeping his distance for days, and while there'd been a time when she'd thought she would appreciate that, she now knew she'd been wrong.

And since his kindness with Darcy, his quick thinking with Truman's high-wire act, his purchase of the teapot, and that damnable whatever it was about him that made her want and need him, she knew it was time to make *her* move—that was, if she hadn't discouraged him with her mercurial moods and her two-year-old grudge.

Amy panicked halfway through the party when she couldn't find Tom. Moments ago she'd seen him dancing with Jo, then Karma had cut in, and now he seemed to have disappeared.

The party had spilled out into all the other downstairs rooms, and she checked them all, wondering if he'd just gone looking for a comfortable place to sit out the tango now blaring from the disc player.

But he wasn't there. She slipped outside to see if he'd simply needed air. She encountered the two straw figures Diantha made every year and placed on her porch swing, jack-o'-lanterns on the stairs, and a harem dancer and a cowboy, late arrivals to the party. But no Tom.

Just her luck, she thought. She'd finally decided to do something positive about their relationship—and picked the moment he'd apparently decided to forget the whole thing.

She wandered down the steps and onto the gravel walk, a frosty moon lighting her way. The smell of wood smoke filled the air, along with the fresh and salty tang of Katherine's Bay on the other side of the road. She heard the lap of water, the stir of a light wind in the trees.

This town, she thought, opening her arms in an unconscious effort to embrace it, had given her everything she'd ever wanted in the way of friendships and a sense of purpose and belonging. But without Tom there was a bittersweetness about it.

Amy picked up her skirts, prepared to walk a little farther, when a call from the direction of the house stopped her.

"Aimée!"

She whirled, the very sound of Tom's voice filling her chest with a warmth that suddenly seemed to clarify everything. And he's used the French pronunciation of her name, which meant "beloved."

He came down the steps toward her, a tall, broad silhouette in his seventeenth-century clothes. In the darkness, the white plume of his hat fluttered, and his cape billowed out behind him as he came toward her.

The sword bumped against his leg, and the leather of his boots bit the gravel. She had the strangest sense of being lost in literary fiction.

"Monsieur?" she asked.

"Ladies are not permitted to wander the grounds at night unescorted," he said as he approached.

"But I set out to find you, sir." She looked up at him, trying to read his eyes in the shadows. "Were you hiding from me?"

"Not at all," he replied. "I brought in wood for the mistress of our...inn." He swept a lace-cuffed wrist toward Diantha's home, warmly lit against the dark. "When I returned, my comrades told me you'd gone out without an escort."

"My escort," she said, "was apparently busy seeing to the needs of another lady."

They stared at each other for a moment, a man and a woman in seventeenth-century dress under a harvest moon, hearing clearly everything that wasn't being said.

Tom put a hand to the hilt of his sword and shifted his weight. "My apologies, *mademoiselle*," he said quietly. "You wished for an escort to take a walk in the dark?"

Amy wound her arms around his neck and reached up on tiptoe until her mouth was a fraction of an inch from his. "No, *monsieur*. I wish you would escort me home."

"Amy..."

"Please."

The fictional spell broken, the night became suddenly very real.

Tom ripped off the hat and wig and mustache. And the air of gentlemanly courtesy.

"No more theatrics, Amy," he warned. "I am so tired of dancing around the issue. D'Artagnan has left the building. Do you want Tom Nicholas to take you home?"

Amy kissed him slowly, dipping into his mouth with the tip of her tongue, nipping at his lip, kissing a path to his ear. "I want Tom Nicholas to make love with me tonight," she whispered.

Tom didn't give her time for second thoughts. He whipped the cape off and wrapped it around her. Then he lifted her into his arms, carried her to his truck and headed for her house.

"We should have told someone we were leaving," Amy said softly as she fumbled in her very twentieth-century purse for her key in the meager light of her front porch.

"Everyone will have figured it out," Tom assured her. "They know more about us than we do. Would it be easier for me to break a window?"

"Got it." She turned the key in the lock and pushed the door in, then waited for him to follow her inside and locked it behind him.

The instant she turned away from the door, he had her in his arms. He carried her upstairs to her bedroom, carefully skirting the table in the hallway. There was a new pot on it, holding the familiar eucalyptus.

A light she'd left on in the hall illuminated the foot of a four-poster with a crocheted spread and canopy.

He set her on her feet and smiled at their surroundings. "It's almost too bad we left d'Artagnan behind. He probably would have felt right at home here."

Amy pushed him lightly until he sat on the edge of the bed, then she turned her back to him and drew up his right leg to pull off the boot.

He planted his other boot against the seat of her skirt and pushed.

She turned back to him with a smile of surprise. "It amazes me that that works. You see that in movies all the time, and it seems so...I don't know..."

"Indelicate?" he suggested.

"Yes." She turned again and raised his other leg. She handled it carefully. This was the one that had been badly burned and that had given him so much trouble. To relieve any discomfort he might feel, she chattered on. "I mean, can you imagine being engaged in a dalliance for the first time, setting the scene in some romantic hunting lodge or something, and having the gentleman kick the lady halfway across the room in the process of removing his boots?"

"Believe it or not," he said, leaning back on his elbows and planting his boot very lightly on her, "I haven't given that much thought. But it is essential to get the boots off. I mean, how many ladies would want them on their lovely linens? Of course, there's the option of making love on the carpeting, or in the hayloft. Then he could leave his boots on."

She pulled off the second boot, then turned to him, laughing. "Do you suppose *that's* why love is made so often in haylofts?"

He sat up, caught her waist and brought her down

beside him. Then he knelt astride her, prepared to undress her. But there were no buttons or zippers that he could see.

"While you were considering the delicate problem of the gentleman's boot on the lady's derriere," he said, grinning down at her, "did you come to a solution for the gentleman eventually uncovering said derriere?"

She laughed again. "The top is laced up the back," she said. "And the skirt is separate."

She turned over, brushing the inside of his thigh and that part of him already aching for her. He lost his breath, his ability to joke.

He unlaced the top and found a bow at the back of her skirt that was easily untied. Bracing his hands on the mattress on either side of her, he slipped backward off the bed and pulled off the skirt and a pair of little silky slippers. Then she sat up and he helped her remove the top.

Her breasts rose beautifully out of a corset so tight that it made him wince just looking at it. Then his attention was caught by a pair of white undies that looked like bloomers with a slip attached.

"Petticoat breeches," she said, her voice sounding a little high.

His hand went to the front laces of the corset. "Let's get this instrument of torture off first."

"You undo the back laces," she said, turning her back to him. He got her out of it, then tipped her backward onto the bed and pulled off the fussy bloomers.

"So I guess the man who remained interested after all that," she said, her ivory body lying on the lace like some very artful pattern in it, "deserved the lady's charms."

The breath caught in his throat, and he felt his blood

thicken at the sight of her full, beautiful breasts, her narrow waist, the very feminine flare of hip and length of thigh. He felt awed and reverent all at once.

He groaned her name and leaned over her to plant a kiss at her throat.

They'd gotten this far before, he remembered, with the sense of that having been in another lifetime. Then she'd touched his bad leg, he'd gone a little crazy, they'd shouted at each other and he'd gathered up his clothes and stalked away.

But he was different now, and that made this all new. And he wanted to make up to her for the last time.

He pulled his belt and sword off and tossed them onto the floor. He was working competently at the tiny buttons on his doublet, until she put her hands to his waist to unfasten his breeches and he seemed to lose all coordination.

He regained it again when she knelt up on the bed and slipped her hands between his flesh and the out-of-character Joe Boxers he wore under the breeches and whispered, "Oh, Tom. I've waited so long for this."

In a moment they were naked in the middle of the bed. She had tossed the coverlet back and they lay on sheets that were soft against his skin—flannel, he guessed. The air was cool but he was at the point of combustion.

He tucked her into his right arm, and with his left hand he explored every rise and hollow of her body, every beautiful curve and every musky secret.

Her hands moved over him tenderly, but with a boldness that surprised and flattered him. He felt her breath against his shoulder, sometimes deep and content, sometimes coming in shallow little puffs, depending on where she touched.

Her fingertips ran over his ribs, into the indentation of his waist, then over his stomach. Then they detoured from where he wanted them to his leg—the bad one.

She stopped at the juncture of thigh and torso, just where the scars began, and turned her face to look into his eyes.

"I've loved you for a long time, Tom," she whispered. "And I've loved all of you—good leg, bad leg, good moods, bad moods...." She smiled and kissed his nipple. "Nothing about you is ugly to me. The scars on your leg are just a reminder that you were willing to risk your life for someone in danger. And your grief over Davey defines that part of you that wants to do more and be more than anyone ever expects of you."

She drew her hand up to wrap it around his waist as she lay her head on his chest. "And I want—all I ever wanted—was to be allowed in. Let me share what you feel, whatever it is. And let me love who you are, scars and all. All right?"

He almost didn't have the voice to answer. He had to swallow and accept that he would never belong to himself again. "All right," he said finally.

She braced herself to kiss his mouth, then pushed herself down his body until she could explore his leg with lips and fingertips.

Amy felt the hard ridges of scars from the top of his thigh to the soles of his foot. The part of her that knew his anguish and felt his pain wanted to scream with the image of the agony he'd experienced in that minute when his leg had been trapped under a burning wall.

She put her lips to the tracery of scars, repeating with kisses and the gentle strokes of her fingertips everything she'd told him earlier—that all of him was beautiful to her.

She breathed love words and kisses over his knee and down his shinbone, then up again. Then she kissed the firm length of his manhood.

Tom experienced the benediction of her healing kisses on his leg, then his heart jolted to a stop when she kissed his eager erection. In that split second the anguish of two long years was erased, and the future he'd thought was lost reappeared.

But his need was urgent, imminent. And he didn't want to lose her in this wondrous second chance.

He caught her shoulders and pulled her down beside him. She wrapped her arms around him, breasts straining against his chest. He reached gently inside her, gritting his teeth against his own need to take time to prepare her for him.

But she was ready, opening for him, straining up to him.

He entered her swiftly, deeply, and held there as she enfolded him with a little moan he might have interpreted as pain if she hadn't held so tightly to him, wrapped her legs around him and tightened on him like a tide-pool flower.

He groaned, too, with the exquisite pleasure.

Amy felt as though she'd gained a new dimension. While trapped between promise and pleasure, she waited, wrapped deliciously in his arms. She could feel every muscle in his body in contact with hers, every pore absorb his breath, felt the hair on his chest abrading the tips of her breasts and causing a conflagration at the waiting heart of her.

Tom moved gently out of her, then in again with possessive confidence. He withdrew and returned again and again until the tightening tension made her wild.

He thrust again as she rose to him and her world

ignited. Everything familiar flew apart, and everything she'd ever wished for came together. It was like rebirth, she thought, some quiet part of her brain still functioning in the explosion of sensation.

She trembled inside and out. Sparks raced along her veins toward a powder keg of feeling, but instead of destroying her, the flames seemed to race back to their source and build warmth there.

She felt like Venus rising out of the sea. Or like the woman whose teapot she owned must have felt when she turned around in the rubble of her old life and found the carpenter standing there.

Everything was new again.

THE TROUBLE BEGAN about 3:00 a.m. Amy sat in a robe in front of the fireplace and Tom lay propped on his elbow beside her in a pair of sweats he'd retrieved from his gym bag in the truck. They were sharing a sandwich she'd made and a bottle of merlot she'd received as a birthday gift months ago and never opened.

"I was thinking," Tom said, topping up their glasses with the wine, "that when the barn's finished, we could take the *Mud Hen* out for a week or so before we get caught up in the holiday confusion."

She sipped at her wine, loving the idea of a week alone with him. Reality, however, had to prevail. "That sounds wonderful." She passed a large slice of spicy pickle from her plate to his. "But I'm fixing up the barn because I have a waiting list of children."

He met her gaze and asked reasonably, "But they've been waiting all this time. Would one more week make that much difference?"

"Well…" It probably wouldn't, but the whole point of doing this from the beginning had been to make it a success, to serve as many families as wanted to use her services. "What about the children who come regularly now?"

"Couldn't they make other arrangements for a week?" he insisted quietly. "Three of them belong to Jave and Nancy, and they only come a couple of days. I imagine they could work something out. And certainly the others would understand your need for a week's break."

Amy was experiencing a mild sense of panic she didn't entirely understand. Kids & Co. had become her identity, it was the first thing she'd done entirely on her own, and it was succeeding beyond her expectations. And it would thrill her enormously to see it become bigger and better.

If this expansion proved profitable, she was considering opening a branch in Seaside, down the coast. For the first time in her life she could hold her head up among her successful family members. Granted, it wasn't a courtroom or Hollywood, but it was her own.

She tried to explain that to Tom.

He listened to her patiently, his expression growing more and more unreadable as she went on.

"Amy, we're talking about seven days," he said when she'd finally finished. "I know you have this need to compete with your sisters, but don't you want a life that isn't governed by them?"

She frowned, confused. "What do you mean? That's why I came to Heron Point."

"Amy, moving didn't do it." His tone was losing some of its quiet reasonableness. "You're still ruled by the need to do your sisters one better. Don't you want anything besides that? Don't you have some personal goals that don't involve familial revenge?"

"It isn't revenge," she disputed. "It's…I don't know. I guess I have to know that I measure up."

"To whom? All you have to be is who *you* are."

She stood impatiently and paced across the room. "You're very philosophical for someone who had to run away from his problems."

Tom sat up slowly, eyes darkening. "I went away to straighten myself out. I'd lived with guilt so long, I was no longer sure who I was without it. But I found out. Still me—not perfect, not awful, just me. And that's all I want from you—not some day-care mogul with branches in fifty states. Just Amy—who makes every little kid feel special."

She appreciated his simple assessment, but she had things to prove, and he had to understand that. "You told me you went away because you had to understand yourself before you could be anything to me. Well, I'm the same. I'm the new, improved Amy, and I have to know that I have no limits. Particularly any set by someone else."

He got to his feet but remained where he stood as she marched past him in her agitated pacing. Her shoulder brushed his. She felt his stiffness, his anger.

"What you're telling me," he assessed, "is that you're not making any concessions to me. If that's the case, then why is it so important to get inside me, to 'be allowed in' as you put it, if what I'm feeling doesn't matter to you?"

"I'm telling you," she corrected him, straining to make him understand, "that I want to build the day care and make it the best one around."

"You're not interested in a personal life beyond the occasional blanket waltz after a party, then?"

The question was asked lightly, diminishing the significance of all that had gone before during the night.

She wanted very much to hit him. Instead, she fixed him with a look of disdain. "I think this conversation is deteriorating beyond redemption. Don't get holier than thou with me about our relationship. It was second to what *you* needed two years ago."

He caught her arm and pulled her to him, his face set in tight, angry lines. "No. It was first, and that was why I left. But you don't seem to understand that no matter how often I say it, so I guess you're right. This conversation—just like this relationship—is going nowhere." The silence ticked as he dropped his hands from her and grabbed his keys from the coffee table. "I'll finish the job, and then I'm out of here. The best thing you can do for me in the interim is stay out of my way."

"That will be my pleasure!" she shouted after him as he slammed the front door behind him.

Chapter Nine

Amy rose Friday morning with a throbbing headache and the sense of oppression that always accompanied the first few waking moments of the day after a tragedy. But it wasn't a tragedy, she told herself bracingly. She'd survived before and she could do it again.

She glanced at the bedside clock and groaned. She was half an hour later than usual, and this was going to be a day that required she have all her wits about her.

She had all three September 23 babies for the entire weekend. Their fathers were in Portland for a workshop on new medical equipment—Jave and Nate representing the hospital, and Ryan as a member of the hospital board.

When Amy had heard their wives speculate dreamily over the opportunity to accompany them and do some early Christmas shopping, she volunteered to watch the babies free of charge, not as their day-care provider, but as their friend.

"But we wouldn't be back until Monday night," Nancy said, her protest halfhearted.

Amy had shrugged. "No problem."

But that had been before the argument with Tom had snapped her spirit in two.

All the after-school kids would be coming today, as well as several drop-ins. She and Kate would be tried to their limits.

The whine of a saw came from the direction of the barn, and an echoing cry tried to form inside her. But she pushed it away.

She was doing fine. She would continue to be fine.

She swung her legs out of bed and stepped down onto the carpet, prepared to sprint to the shower and jump into her clothes.

But her feet connected with something metallic and cold, and she looked down in surprise, wondering what it was.

There, still trapped in the leather-worked baldric that had strapped them to Tom's waist, were the sword and scabbard he'd discarded last night just before he'd made love to her.

She managed to step over it and head for the shower, but she sobbed all the way.

THERE WAS NOTHING like a house filled with children, she thought by the middle of the afternoon, to force a woman to rise to the occasion. She dispensed meals, hugs, cautions, Band-Aids, toys and treats with an efficiency that made even Kate take notice.

"What's with you today?" she asked while the babies napped in the afternoon. "You're like a madwoman, but a sort of…robotic one. Repressed anxiety? Unresolved anger? Unrequited love?"

Amy ignored her questions and handed her a fresh box of disposable diapers to put away. Nothing seemed to matter much except that the children's needs were seen to and that the whine continued from the direction of the barn.

She had a sudden fear that Tom might wander in for a glass of water or a cup of coffee as he'd gotten in the habit of doing, and that she would burst into tears.

She hadn't shed one since she'd come out of the shower, but she felt as though they were just behind her eyes, a sob waiting in her throat.

But as long as the saw was whining, she knew Tom was a safe distance away.

The after-school kids arrived in a rowdy mood, high, she guessed, on all the Halloween candy they'd devoured. It was also another rare sunny fall day, and they were pushing and shoving one another, obviously in an outdoor mood. They showed off for the drop-in kids, a brother and a sister who were Truman's and Rodney's ages, but far less rambunctious.

The girl was happy to play dolls with Darcy, though it took some explaining for her to understand why one of the dolls was still in its original box and had to remain there. But when Darcy gave her the other doll to play with, she didn't care.

The boy went out to play on the monkey bars with the others, then returned a while later and busied himself with Legos on the coffee table.

Mercifully, the babies slept on.

Amy had mopped up a glass of juice Darcy had spilled and was emptying her wet-dry vac when she suddenly noticed the silence. She went to the window over the kitchen sink and looked out at the monkey bars and found them empty.

She put the vac down and went to the back door and yanked it open. The slide was empty, there was no one on the teeter-totter, and the swings dangled in the afternoon breeze.

Amy shouted to Kate. "Have you seen the boys?"

Kate came around the corner of the kitchen. "They were on the monkey bars a few minutes ago." She looked over Amy's shoulder into the empty backyard. "I'll check out the front."

She hurried off and was back a moment later. "Not there," she said. "I know you've insisted that they not bother Tom, but you know how he invites them into the barn sometimes."

"Tom's truck left half an hour ago," Amy said. "He must have gone for supplies or to get something to eat." Then a horrible thought struck her. It was possible the boys had gone to the barn to investigate his tools without someone cautioning them not to touch this or that, not to press buttons or flip switches.

There was a cry from the nap room. One of the babies was awake. That meant they would all be up in a minute.

"I'm going to run out to the barn," Amy said. "Will you be all right alone for a few minutes?"

"Sure." Kate shooed her out the door. "I'll feed the little ones and they'll be fine. The other kids are all busy."

Amy ran across the field to the barn, unable to shake a sense of foreboding. She put it down to the grimness of her state of mind after her argument with Tom and told herself that the boys would be in the barn, simply eager to look over the tools.

But they weren't there. She looked upstairs, just to cover all bases, and felt a stab of fear when she didn't see them.

She couldn't imagine where they could have gone. They knew the woods were off-limits. But they were preadolescent boys, she reminded herself, a completely unpredictable species. And they were in a rowdy mood today. It was entirely possible that they'd chosen to ignore the rules and go exploring.

She ran down the stairs and across the barn to the door, where she was almost impaled by a length of molding.

Tom shouted a warning and she darted aside.

"You didn't take the boys to the lumberyard with you, did you?" she demanded anxiously.

It sounded like a sarcastic question, and she saw him set the molding down and prepare to answer in the same tone—and then he looked into her eyes and his expression changed.

"No," he replied. "Why? What's wrong?"

"They're missing," she said, pushing past him to step outside. "I've looked everywhere. All that's left is the woods, but they know they're not supposed to go in. They were feeling their oats today, though, so they might have decided to do it, anyway."

"Who's missing?"

"The four boys. Your nephews, and Rodney and Truman."

He rolled his eyes. "All right. I'll help you look." He pointed to the trail right behind the barn. "You know where the stream is just before you get to the road?"

"Yes."

"You follow this trail to the stream. I'll take the one that starts at the other edge of the woods. Deer come out of there all the time, and they might have spotted one and followed it in. I'll meet you at the stream."

Amy didn't wait to discuss it any longer. She walked at a brisk pace, but stopped to listen every few minutes, convinced that four boys between the ages of eight and twelve could be neither invisible nor inaudible.

But she didn't see them, and she didn't hear a sound that didn't belong to the woods. Wings flapped, things scurried, insects buzzed—and there was that eerie sense of being watched by eyes that couldn't be seen.

She walked on, careful of her footing as roots rose out of the muddy path and ferns and vines reached out for her.

Tom felt like a boiling cauldron of anger, fear and regret.

Uppermost was fear. Reason told him that his nephews were capable and competent boys who usually knew better than to flout the rules. But Eddy was growing more adventurous with age, and Pete was determined to keep up with him. Truman was a wild card the equation didn't need, and Rodney, despite his propensity for swear words, was happy to go along with anyone on anything.

Tom prayed that it was simply adventure that had drawn them, and not one of the dozens of nameless evils that preyed on children—even in cozy little Heron Point.

His anger might have been explained as a normal response to a situation he couldn't control, but it had already been alive in him when he'd found Amy in the barn with that frightened look on her face.

Anger had been bristling in him since their argument in the early hours of the morning, but had been nicely fanned by the possibility that Eddy and Pete had taken off on a lark when their parents were a hundred miles away.

He really didn't understand the regret. It was just there. He didn't know why he should regret the loss of a woman who didn't particularly want to spend time with him—unless it was the memory of her making love with him last night like a woman obsessed.

He put emotions out of his mind and tried to concentrate on several sets of boy-sized footprints. They seemed to step all over one another, then move off the trail and into the trees. They were lost completely in the thick underbrush, so he stayed with the trail, eyes and ears scanning as he moved.

He was almost to the stream when he heard the sound of excited voices and a growl that didn't sound quite doglike. He recognized it instantly.

Raccoons fought over cat food left out overnight in his mother's neighborhood. They were beautiful creatures and generally harmless, but every once in a while there was one with an attitude.

And as Tom came upon the boys and Amy on the edge of the stream, he understood what had upset this particular raccoon. The odds were it was a female, and the small raccoon Amy held in her hands was its baby.

The mother raccoon was inches from her, teeth bared as it gave her its demon-from-hell growl. The boys fanned out around her, and Eddy was poking at the mother with a stick when it got too close. Amy was inspecting something on the baby raccoon's foot.

"Put it down!" Tom shouted at her as he came through the trees.

She glanced up at him, her eyes startled, but she continued to work on the small raccoon's foot.

The mother raccoon charged again, but Eddy beat it back. It parried with his stick on its hind legs, its teeth bared in a vicious snarl.

Tom, imagining the raccoon leaping onto Amy after its baby, cleared the few yards that still separated them, snatched the baby from her and tossed it low on the ground toward its mother. Mother and baby disappeared into the underbrush, the mother still snarling and scolding.

Tom turned to the boys and Amy, anger now definitely uppermost. Amy's face and Eddy's wrist were scratched, and Truman had scratches on both hands.

Eddy and Pete looked up at him, eyes wide and uncertain, then Eddy turned back to Amy. "Did you get it?" he asked.

She held up a two-inch length of blackberry stem with its vicious thorns.

The boys cheered and Amy grinned.

Tom felt on the brink of apoplexy.

"Eddy," he said deliberately, trying to control his voice, though he kept his hands on his hips to withstand the temptation to use them in a throttling motion. The only thing that truly prevented him was that he didn't know whose teeth to rattle first—the boys who'd obviously disobeyed the directive about the woods, or Amy, who'd stopped to do first aid on a baby raccoon while its mother charged her. "I'd like to know why you guys ignored Amy's rule about the woods."

Eddy swallowed. "You left," he said quickly, "and we went to the barn to look in at your stuff. Just to look!" he added on a defensive note when Tom's gaze narrowed on him. "We didn't touch anything. Then we saw the mother raccoon and two babies running across the field toward the woods. One of the babies was limping. So we went in after it."

"The woods are off-limits," Tom reminded him.

Truman frowned at him. "The baby was limping," he repeated Eddy's words.

"So we followed them," Eddy went on, giving Tom a judicious look. "Dad's a doctor. He'd understand."

Tom doubted it seriously. He'd seen Jave in action when the boys had behaved recklessly, and it wasn't for the fainthearted.

"You could have been hurt!" Tom said quietly but firmly. "I can't believe you boys haven't seen enough nature films to know that wild animal mothers don't stop to analyze if you're helping or hurting their babies. All they know is that you've got them and they want them back!" He turned to Amy. "And you had to hold it?"

She glared at him and opened her mouth to reply, but Truman came instantly to her defense. "I picked the baby up. She took it from me when the mother tried to jump at me."

"Then Eddy got the stick," Rodney said excitedly, "and held the damn thing off!" When Amy and Tom both turned to him he took a step back and amended more quietly, "Sorry. The darn thing."

"Yeah! It was so cool, Uncle Tom!" Pete added. "It coulda got an infection or something, but we saved it! Just like Dad or Uncle Nate!"

"You listen to me," he said, focusing on one boy, then the next, until he had the undivided attention of all four pairs of eyes. "You boys got really lucky that Amy found you in time, otherwise the raccoon could have really hurt you. You should not have come into the woods in the first place. Amy put it off-limits, and when you're here, she's the boss! In the second place, *never* pick up a wild animal, even if it looks cute and cuddly. Raccoons have long nails and strong teeth! And I don't think we have the problem in Oregon, but a lot of times they have rabies!"

"You have to get shots in the gut for that!" Rodney

said, as though the idea had serious appeal. "It hurts like hell! Heck, I mean!"

Eddy shook his head and told Tom defensively, "They don't do that anymore. There's a new way that isn't so bad."

Tom held his stare. "That's not the point, Eddy."

Eddy sighed. "I know. We just felt bad seeing the little guy limp." His eyes reminded Tom suddenly, startlingly, of Jave's. "Like when you used to limp. It was like I could feel it, even though it was on you and not on me."

For a moment Tom was speechless. And during that time he could feel Amy's gaze boring a hole into him. He ignored it.

"It's great that you guys wanted to help," he said finally. "But I think all your dads would be pretty upset. I think they would rather have you safe than the raccoon."

For the first time since he'd found Amy in the barn, Tom noticed that she hadn't stopped to put on a jacket, and that there was gooseflesh on her arms and she was trembling.

"Let's get back to the house," he said to the boys. Then he pulled off his denim jacket and held it open for Amy.

"I'm fine, thank you," she said stiffly, and tried to move past him.

He caught her arm and forced it into a sleeve. "Don't act like a brat in front of the boys," he said under his breath.

She jammed her arm into the other sleeve, pulled away from him and fell in line between Eddy and Rodney as they headed back up the trail. Pete followed her.

Truman kept pace with Tom.

"I think it would be all right with my dad," he said, looking up at Tom through the long blond hair falling over his eyes, "if something happened to me."

Edgy and irritable, Tom shook his head and turned his attention to the trail. "That's ridiculous, Truman. And you know it."

"No, it's true," the boy said seriously. "He tries to pretend, but I know he doesn't like me anymore."

"Truman…"

"My mom died because of me," Truman blurted out, his voice alarmingly matter-of-fact.

But when Tom stopped in his tracks and Truman looked up at him, Tom saw that his eyes had filled and his bottom lip trembled dangerously.

"Truman." Tom put his hands on his shoulders and leaned down to him. "That isn't true. You told me she had cancer."

He tried to speak, but a choked sob came out instead. Then he drew a breath and tried again. "Because…she always used to say, 'Truman, someday you'll be the death of me.'" He shrugged a shoulder and a tear fell onto his dirty cheek. "And then I was."

Tom felt Truman's pain go right through him. He shook him gently, then said with all the conviction he could collect, "No, you were not. She died because sometimes cancer is big, bad stuff and even doctors with all the best medicines and treatment have trouble fighting it. It wasn't because of anything you did."

Truman dragged the sleeve of his flannel jacket across his eyes. "But maybe she got it 'cause she worried about the things I did."

"No. That can't happen, Truman. They're not always sure what makes somebody get it, but something your body can't fight gets inside it and takes over. But you can't get it from worry about somebody. Absolutely not.''

Truman considered that, then shook his head. ''But she said...''

''No. That's just an expression. When parents love their kids a lot, they tell them that so they'll stop doing things that worry them. You didn't do it. The cancer did.''

Truman thought about that, then frowned, apparently concentrating on the differences between how he'd thought things were and how they might be. ''Are you sure?'' he asked doubtfully.

''You know what I think we should do,'' Tom suggested, eager to hold on to the small advance he thought he was making here. ''My brother, Eddy and Pete's dad, is a radiologist. You know what that is?''

Truman nodded. ''He takes pictures of your guts.''

That was close enough. ''Right. I think you and your dad should go talk to him. He helps people who have cancer, and he can tell you how it works, that one person can't make another person get it. Okay? But he's in Portland for the weekend, so it'll have to be next week, okay?''

''Yeah,'' Truman said. ''We're all going on a Boy Scout camp-out. Rodney's dad is gonna take us all home with him tonight.''

''Right.'' When Tom had volunteered to keep the boys for the weekend, Jave had told him about the camp-out. ''Well, we'll talk to him about it when he comes back.''

Truman's eyes were still worried. ''Okay.''

''But until then,'' Tom said, holding the boy to him for a moment, ''you can be sure your dad loves you very much.''

"How do you know?"

"Amy told me."

That seemed to put the issue into a believable area for him. Because Amy said so.

Tom led him back to the house.

When they arrived, Boomer was there to pick up the boys, and Amy gave Tom another glare when he straggled in with Truman. She had the boys' camping gear stashed in the kitchen, and doubled-checked that they had everything before they left. Apparently she hadn't said anything about the raccoon.

The boys watched Tom apprehensively as he shook hands with Boomer and exchanged waterfront gossip. But he went out onto the front porch with Amy to wave them off without mentioning the raccoon incident.

Amy ripped into him the moment the car was out of the driveway.

"This is *my* day care!" she roared at him, pointing her finger at him, except that it had little impact because it barely protruded from the long sleeve of his jacket. "Don't you *ever* take over like that again!"

"You asked *me* for help," he retorted.

"I know you snarled because you were frightened for your nephews, but can't you ever correct children without jumping on them with both feet! They're not nails you hammer in until they're in place, they're boys who have malleable, impressionable, suggestible little minds that can be turned in the wrong direction so fast...."

That was true. Truman had just borne that out.

He caught the hand, or rather the sleeve with which she now jabbed him in the shoulder, and held it still. "Amy, those boys are smart and inquisitive. If you aren't more firm with them and don't make them accountable when they don't listen, they'll do themselves harm.''

"Can you really scold them," she demanded, "for wanting to help an injured animal?"

"Yes!" he shouted back at her. "Or didn't you see the mother snapping and snarling at you?"

Amy knew he was right, but she was so angry at him at the moment for so many different things—personal and professional—she felt obliged to stand against him, whatever the issue.

Then she noticed a subtle shift in his mood. His frown deepened. "Incidentally, are you aware that Truman considers himself responsible for his mother's death?''

Amy had to stare at him for a moment while she tried to comprehend the question. "What? How?''

"Apparently she used an unfortunate choice of words. She used to tell him he was going to be the death of her.'' Tom shook his head. "My mother *always* said that to me. Only in Truman's case—she did die. And in his child's brain he thinks it means he *did* become the death of her. I think you should tell Fuller about it. He's probably not aware of it, either. I told Truman he should talk to Jave when he gets back. He'll be able to put it in terms that should put Truman's mind at ease.''

Then Tom's mood changed again, and he freed her hand and said with male arrogance, "I don't see how you can in all conscience consider expanding to accept more children when you don't understand and can't control the ones you already have.''

Then he walked around the house and back to the barn.

Amy was torn between wanting to kill him and wanting to bludgeon herself. Poor Truman! She'd suspected that his grief over his mother was partially responsible for his recklessness, but she'd had no idea he blamed himself for her death. And she felt that she'd failed him, somehow, because he hadn't confided that to her.

She helped the babies play with big wooden puzzles while Darcy and the two walk-ins played Old Maid at the kitchen table. But her mind kept going first to Truman, then to the fact that she'd allowed the boys to slip away from her. It was easy for parents to comfort each other when children did reckless things by saying that they were quick, that even the most vigilant parent could miss a child's move toward potential danger.

But when that child was being watched by a child-care professional, there were no excuses that applied. Her job was to watch them at all times even more vigilantly than a parent would.

So in a sense, Tom was right. But she refused to even think about him. Love that had turned to anger was a corrosive thing, particularly when it came around a second time.

The walk-ins' mother arrived just before five. Amy was gratified when the children told their mother they'd love to come again.

"I'd like to come all the time!" the boy said with sudden animation. "The other guys got to see all the carpenter's power tools and saved a whole family of raccoons from a bear!"

When the boy began to talk, Amy closed her eyes, certain her new client-care provider relationship with their mother was about to go down the tubes. Fortunately, the exaggeration and bravado with which the story had apparently been told by the other boys ultimately saved her.

The children's mother smiled, apparently put the

story down to exaggeration and told the boy to put on his jacket. She paid Amy and promised her she would check her calendar and set a formal schedule for the rest of the month.

Amy privately applauded her lucky escape, and her foresight in renovating the barn. But that brought back thoughts of Tom, so she busied herself helping Darcy put the cards away.

Steve Fuller arrived a few moments later. Amy held the door open for him in surprise. "Did you forget that Truman was going away for the weekend?" she asked.

He laughed lightly. "Hardly. I just wanted to make sure the boys got off okay."

"Yes," she replied. "About half an hour ago. Come in. I'll pour you a cup of coffee. I'd like to talk to you about Truman."

Steve winced. "What did he do?"

She smiled and pointed him to the kitchen table. If Tom wasn't saying anything about the raccoon rescue, she wouldn't, either. "Let me put a tape in for Darcy and I'll be right there."

The babies were busy with a PlaySkool slide she kept in a corner of the living room. She could watch them easily from the kitchen table.

She poured Steve a cup of coffee and sat across from him with her own and told him what Tom had told her. He stared at her, just as she'd stared at Tom.

"But…it's just an expression!" he said. "She also used to tell *me* that all the time."

"Well, you know, kids are very literal. He'd probably like to know that she said the same thing to you."

"But, I…" He was clearly upset.

Amy patted his arm. "It's hard to know what's going on in a child's mind. Don't beat yourself up because you didn't see it. I didn't, either, and I'm supposed to be trained to do this. And he functions very well, he just has a propensity for danger that might diminish if he was sure you didn't blame him for anything. Tom suggested you take him to see Jave Nicholas. That he can explain to Truman that what he thinks happened is impossible.''

Steve closed his eyes and let his head fall back, a sound of anguish escaping him. ''God. I can't believe this.''

''What? What happened?'' Darcy's mother had let herself in as she often did when the noise level in the house was high and she didn't think her knock would be heard. She came to the table. ''Is something wrong with Truman?''

Steve had both hands over his face. Ginger sat down beside him and put a hand on his shoulder.

''Truman's all right,'' Amy said, getting up to pour another cup of coffee. ''He just…misunderstood something about his mother's death.''

Unsure how much Steve would want to reveal, Amy had answered Ginger carefully, then sat back in surprise when Ginger leaned toward Steve and asked quietly, ''Do you want to talk about it? There's nothing scarier than raising a child by yourself, is there?''

Steve lowered his hands and drew a deep breath. ''It makes me feel like a complete incompetent.''

Ginger nodded. ''Been there. In fact, I'm still there.'' She smiled at him. ''Darcy and I are going for pizza tonight. Since Truman's with the Scouts this weekend, you want to come with us? We can cry on each other's shoulder while Darcy plays video games.''

Steve blinked once, as though he wasn't certain he'd

comprehended the question. Then he nodded slowly. "Yes," he said finally. "Pizza sounds good."

They were gone in a matter of minutes. Amy watched Ginger drive off, Steve pulling onto the road behind her, and wondered if anyone else had ever considered that a day-care business could provide parent care and a dating service, as well.

"Okay, babies," she said, closing and locking the door. "It's just us for the whole weekend. What do you want to do?"

MALIA: Let's go to Darby's Dresses and try on clothes!

CHELSEA: Let's order Chinese takeout and watch *The Sound of Music!*

GARRETT: Bowling!

TOM COULDN'T IMAGINE where Amy was going with three two-year-olds, but he told himself he didn't care. She didn't want his help—even when she asked for it— so she could just fend for herself. She was the trained professional, anyway.

He was packing his truck two hours later when she returned, holding Garrett between her knees and Chelsea by the arm as she released Malia from her car seat.

Apparently just fed, they were even harder to keep tabs on than usual. But before they could scatter on her, she picked up Garrett, the explorer, anchored Malia by the hand because she was used to running with her brothers, and controlled Chelsea, the mellow one, with her voice.

She had them back in the house in a couple of minutes. He had to give her credit. He also regretted his remark earlier about being unable to control the kids she had. He'd known it wasn't fair when he'd said it, but he'd been mad as hell at her for other reasons, and it had been a convenient way to hurt her. He didn't like knowing he was capable of that.

He would apologize for it, but not tonight. He was still too angry.

He was back at eight in the morning, thinking that he might be able to handle the apology today. He'd slept well, done a couple dozen push-ups this morning, and had a Danish and a cup of coffee in a bag on the seat of the truck.

He'd resolved that things weren't going to come together for him and Amy, so he was going to put it behind him. The barn was going well. He'd finished the floor, installed the new windows and had wallboard up and mudded upstairs and down. One more week of slapping paint and he'd be on to new projects and new women.

He slammed on the brakes when he rounded the back corner of the house and encountered Amy, waving him to a stop. She looked a little rough this morning. Her jeans and shirt were soaked, and her hair tumbled over her eye. She looked as though her composure hung by a thread.

He rolled the window down as she ran around to the driver's side door.

"I'm sorry to stop you before you even get to park the truck," she said, her manner carefully distant. But he could see that desperation lay just under the surface. "The bathroom faucet came off in my hand. I managed to shut off the cutoff valve, but I'm not sure where to go from there. I tried to call a plumber, but all I've gotten so far are answering services. And there's a limit to how long I can go without hot water with three babies in the house.''

''Sure,'' he said, trying to respond with the same neutrality. He liked that she had to ask him for help, but he'd like it better if she acted a little more needy about it. ''No problem.'' He climbed out of the truck, pulled his plumbing tools out of the back and followed her in through the back door.

Three babies in the playpen meant she'd had to keep them out of her hair. He patted heads, then went into the bathroom where a stack of wet towels attested to a mop-up operation.

''I'll get you a cup of coffee,'' she said.

''Thank you,'' he replied, setting to work.

Amy wasn't sure what was wrong with her, but she seemed to be enduring some kind of emotional degeneration. It was happening too slowly to qualify as a collapse, but it was happening.

Last night, when she'd brought the babies home from an excursion to a fast-food place where they'd gotten prizes with their meals, she'd had a revelation. She'd looked at the three beautiful little babies playing on the floor with their bendable animals and wondered if she would spend her entire life looking after someone else's children.

Well, she would, of course. That was the plan. But would she do it without ever having children of her own—children who wouldn't go home with someone else at the end of the day. Children who called her Mom rather than Amy.

And it had gotten slowly but progressively worse from there.

When she'd finally gotten all three babies asleep, she curled up in a corner of the sofa, intent on reading the current Diane Hankins thriller. But she was distracted by the silence.

Usually, she considered silence a blessed thing. But last night it had seemed to scream with loneliness. There were three babies in the next room, she told herself.

"But they're not yours," a hostile inner voice needled.

She'd finally gone to bed and stared at the ceiling for several hours as the feeling of not fitting in that she'd struggled against for so long and thought she'd finally defeated came back to haunt her.

She fought it off. It wasn't her fault that Tom had taken off and left her to find other things to do to make up for the void in her life. It wasn't her fault that the things she'd found to do had served their purpose and now she couldn't just chuck it all—even for a week—to take off with him on a lark.

It *was* her fault, however, that she'd let four little boys wander off into the woods. That she'd shouted at Tom for shouting at them. That she'd known she was wrong but resisted apologizing because she was hurt and angry and didn't want to make that concession.

It *was* her fault that no matter what happened between them, she couldn't seem to see her life without him in it. Even when it stared her emptily in the face as it did in the melancholy darkness of every early morning, she kept thinking about what it would be like if he were there beside her.

She'd finally turned into her pillow and cried herself to sleep. Then Chelsea had awakened, then Garrett, then Malia, and it had taken until almost 4:00 a.m. to get them all back to sleep.

After the long night, she'd gotten up, brushed her teeth and turned on the hot water, intending to put a soothing washcloth on her face, and the faucet had come off and drenched her with warm water in an instant.

And it was just after eight on Saturday morning.

She ran into the bedroom, peeled off her clothes and pulled on a robe, then went into the kitchen for the coffee she'd promised Tom.

She stopped in the bathroom doorway, momentarily paralyzed by the sight of his broad back in a white cotton T-shirt and his trim backside in well-worn jeans as he worked on the faucet with a wrench.

He glanced up into the mirror above the sink and caught her studying him, and she was reminded of their conversation that night in the loft when she'd made light of his warning that Steve intended to make a move on her by admitting that she'd eyed Steve's hips.

He raised an eyebrow.

She put his coffee cup down on the wide windowsill and left the room without a word.

By all indications, it was going to be a very long weekend.

She thought later that she'd had no idea precisely how long until there was a knock on the front door. She looked at the clock, wondering who it could be at this hour. Most of her close friends were out of town, and she'd made it clear to her client parents that having three two-year-olds until Monday evening would make it impossible for her to take any other children until Kate arrived on Monday morning.

She pulled the door open and felt her heart bolt, as though it was trying to hide behind her spinal column.

It wasn't her client parents at all—it was her *real* parents. And her two sisters and her brother-in-law.

She stared at them in stupefaction. They were all supposed to be thousands of miles away—her parents in New York, Peggy on a runway somewhere fashionable, and Jane and Beau winning courtroom battles in Boston.

But they were here in Heron Point. On her doorstep. She prayed for death. Or at least unconsciousness.

Chapter Ten

Amy's mother hugged her, then passed her to her father, and she was transferred from one pair of arms to another until she reached her brother-in-law, who held out his hand. She wasn't offended. She'd seen him greet his own mother with a handshake.

"How are you, Amy?" her mother demanded, her lightly mascaraed, discerning blue eyes going over Amy diagnostically. They widened in horror over her appearance, then rested on her gaze with a look of concern. "It's been so long. I know it's rude to drop in, but *so* much is happening, and we were all just praying you'd be home. Is this...a bad time?"

"Oh, how can it be a bad time?" her father asked in the hale and hearty voice that always dismissed every suggestion of a problem with the insistence that it didn't exist. "Amy's our little ray of sunshine, aren't you, Amy?"

Amy found herself falling into the old pattern, forgetting that she was the new, improved Amy. Her father wanted a little ray of sunshine? She would give him a little ray of sunshine.

"Of course not." Amy opened the door wider. "Come in. Come in."

"What a...quaint old house," her mother said, walking into the living room strewn with toys.

Amy knew her mother didn't really mean it. Sabina Brown had lived too long in a Long Island mansion to appreciate a rundown old Victorian.

In a peacock blue flared knit dress and snakeskin pumps, she picked her way over a PlaySkool train and half the plastic population of Noah's ark, then stopped short at the sight of the playpen and its three inhabitants.

Her sisters followed, Peggy in a winter white bulky sweater, leggings and knee-high boots, her leggy model's body moving with grace and fluidity. Her blond hair was short and chic, her makeup flawless.

Jane, much smaller but just as perfect in a brisk, no-nonsense sort of way, wore a navy-and-white pantsuit, complete with white shirt and tie.

Her father and Beau wore designer suits she knew had probably been purchased from Barney's in New York and Louis's in Boston.

Her mother went into raptures. "Amy! You wrote and said you'd left the hospital and were embarking on a new adventure, but you didn't say what it was!"

"Oh, I..." Amy began.

Her mother turned to her suddenly, putting both hands to her heart and saying in a high whine, "You got married!"

Amy was momentarily distracted by an inability to determine how her mother had come to that conclusion. And before she could respond to it, Peggy said with a roll of her eyes, "Get real, Mom. Didn't you see the sign on the front lawn. It's a day-care center."

"But it's Saturday!" her mother argued.

"So?" Peggy went closer to the playpen to look down at the cherubic little faces looking up at her.

"Lots of people put their children in day care on Saturday. Hi, babies."

"But..." Her mother leaned down to study the babies closely. "These all look to be about the same age. And they're dressed exactly alike. Amy, you've given birth to *triplets?*"

Amy opened her mouth to explain, but Jane said, "Relax, Mom. She isn't married. We haven't been to a wedding, have we? And, anyway—" she patted Amy on the shoulder "—poor Amy is afraid of men."

Amy felt the quicksand of her childhood sucking at her feet. She struggled against it and entertained for just a moment the notion of pretending that these were her babies and that her husband was at work, or on some errand. If she'd been sure they'd only stopped by for an hour, she'd have tried to get away with it, just to see her sisters' looks of surprise.

But that kind of thing always fell apart on one, and she wasn't much of an actress.

Her mother, it seemed, was determined to believe the fantasy Amy couldn't voice.

"But they have the same color hair, except for the bald one. And they all have brown eyes."

Peggy sighed. "Amy's eyes are gray," she said.

"But *his* aren't."

Every head in the room turned toward Jane when she made that observation, then followed the line of her wide-eyed stare to the doorway into the hall where Tom stood, wiping his hands on a towel.

It occurred to Amy that he looked like every uptight woman's secret dream, standing there in white cotton straining across his shoulders, and old jeans clinging to every muscular curve of thigh and calf. His dark good looks stood in dramatic relief above the white shirt.

The casual competence with which he accomplished his task—and the subtly stiff manner he adopted around her as a matter of course—clung to him as he wiped his hands.

Amy's mother and sisters stared. Even Peggy looked back at Amy in disbelief, apparently assuming by the way he'd walked out of the back of the house that he was a love interest.

Her mother looked at the babies, then looked at him and gasped. The babies were all dark like Tom was, and because they were now very used to his presence, they reacted gleefully when he walked into the room. Amy watched in astonishment as her mother's imagination did the rest.

"Amy!" Sabina said on a strangled cry, still staring at Tom. "You...*did* it!"

Amy had no doubt what that unspecific exclamation meant. "You found a man," it said with respectful disbelief. "None of us believed you ever would." She might have been offended at the clear shock on everyone's face, but she was too busy enjoying their near-prostration.

"Amaryllis," her father said briskly. "I think you should introduce us."

"Yes, of course." Amy walked around the playpen toward Tom, enjoying her fantasy for the final few seconds of its life. Then she would introduce Tom to her family as the carpenter who was renovating the barn and explain how he happened to be in the house.

But their thrilled, astounded expressions and cries of admiration continued to fill her awareness, and she realized that for all the "Amy's!" that had been gasped, breathed and shouted, there hadn't been one "*poor*

Amy!'' Because they thought she was married to this man, and that she'd had his three children.

As she reached Tom, she found she just couldn't slough off her family's image of her as a winner—even if it was completely mistaken.

She hooked her arm in Tom's and gave him a look that was half plea, half threat, then turned to her family.

"Everyone, I'd like you to meet my husband, Tom Nicholas, and our children…'' She tugged him toward the playpen so that she could point at each baby as she ticked off their names. She felt the muscle in Tom's arm constrict, and sensed the sharp turn of his head, but she refused to look up at him. "Malia, Chelsea and Garrett. Tom,'' she went on before anyone could interrupt her, "I'd like you to meet my parents, Sabina and Nelson Brown. And my sisters, Peggy Brown and Jane Brown Jones, and her husband, Beau. You all get acquainted, and I'll put on another pot of coffee.''

Sabina flew into Tom's arms with a tearful cry, and Amy turned her back on the scene as everyone else converged on him with offers of shocked and belated congratulations. She hurried to the kitchen, her limbs shaking, her mind screaming, "What are you *doing?*''

She had the coffee going and was microwaving muffins out of the freezer when Tom came into the kitchen.

She started to make a shushing gesture, knowing anything said in a regular tone of voice would be heard in the living room, but he caught her arm and yanked her out the back door. He stopped just outside with her and pulled the door to quietly.

"What *in the hell* do you think you're doing?'' He repeated her mind's question, but with typical male exaggeration.

She was already regretting the impulse, but it had felt so good, she had trouble feeling guilty about it.

"I know, I know," she said, raising both hands in a plea for understanding. "It was stupid and maybe even unforgivable, but I couldn't help it. They were so... shocked when they thought I'd found someone. And you strolled out looking like such a perfect specimen, that for the first time ever, they looked at me with respect. And I just couldn't trade that off for the truth...." She frowned up at him. "That you left me for two whole years and coped just fine without me. That we just can't get it together."

Tom gestured broadly in exasperation. "Amy! You just claimed a husband and children you don't have! These people aren't strangers, they're your family. How long do you think you can keep this up?"

"We probably won't have to for more than a few hours. They do this every couple of years. Somehow all their schedules coincide and they jet in someplace to get together, then they all come to see me because I'm the only one who can't afford to fly anywhere." She sighed ruefully. "We have lunch or dinner together, then they disperse once again, back to their busy lives." She shrugged a shoulder. "It shouldn't be too hard, but you don't owe me anything. If you don't want to cooperate, you don't have to. You can leave, and I'll tell them you had a job to go to or something."

"Or," he said, folding his arms, "I could simply go back inside and tell them the truth."

The thought that her family would be disappointed in her yet again still held all the old horrors. It was demoralizing to know that.

She nodded grimly. "Yes, you could."

He considered her a moment, and she felt her heart fall to her toes as he relished the idea.

"You decided to end a relationship with me," he said, "because you had to prove to yourself that you could be as successful as everyone else in your family. So, in all fairness, I should be able to sacrifice *you* in order to have what I want—which is absolutely no part of this!"

He bristled with anger, and she accepted that she was in all probability facing humiliation in front of her family, followed by alienation from them. It surprised her to feel alarmed by that possibility. She didn't understand them, couldn't relate to them, sometimes didn't like them, and was almost always annoyed by them. But they were her family.

Tom studied her woeful face and knew he couldn't do it. She deserved it, but he was pathetic in his concern for her. And he had overheard some of the conversation from the living room when he'd been wiping down the sink after finishing with the faucet.

He'd heard Peggy's slightly scornful teasing about Amy being afraid of men, and Jane's adamant refusal to even consider that she'd attracted one. If that was indeed a habitual reaction from her sisters, it was no wonder Amy wanted them to believe she was married.

"How do we explain that they weren't invited to the wedding?" he asked. "That you never even wrote and told them you were married? That they have grandchildren? A letter getting lost won't work in this day of cell phones and faxes."

She apparently interpreted his question as a suggestion that he might cooperate and appeared to be racking her brain for a solution. "They'll believe it. They're all generally too busy to keep in close touch except for birthdays and the occasional visit.''

He looked skeptical.

''We could say I was pregnant before we got married,'' she proposed eagerly, ''and was afraid they wouldn't approve?''

''And you wouldn't even have confided in a sister?''

''They don't confide, they compete,'' she said. ''I think they'll believe it.''

He drew a breath, sure he was going to hate himself for this before the two hours were over. ''Okay. But if it all falls apart, *you* have to explain everything. And I'm charging you retail for the leaded-glass window.''

Her eyes closed and she seemed to fall in on herself in relief. Then she opened her eyes and focused on him with a small smile. ''Thank you,'' she whispered. ''I won't forget this.''

She had that right. ''Damn straight you won't,'' he said, and pushed the back door open.

NOT ONLY DID Amy's family seem to swallow the story whole, they fell in love with Tom and the babies.

GARRETT: Hey, this guy's as good as my dad at swinging me around. I wonder how many G's I'm pulling? Who is he, anyway? How come they're acting like they like us so much?

CHELSEA: I wish I was flying. This lady's going to squeeze the life out of me. And she keeps staring at my face. I think it's because Amy's acting like she's our mother and Malia's uncle is our father. Why would they do that? I mean, I know our parents are gone and everything, but usually Amy just baby-sits for us, she doesn't become our mom. You don't think we've been sold, do you?

MALIA: Right. Like anybody, even Amy, would pay to take us. At least your lady seems to like you. Mine keeps staring at me like she's gonna cry. And the man next to her looks like he's afraid of me. I think this is like the Halloween party our parents went to where they pretend to be somebody else. Only this time they're doing it in their own clothes. I'm not sure what it's all about, but Amy will tell us when she has time. She always explains everything to us. Meanwhile, I like the attention. But I wish these two would smile!

AMY CLEARED AWAY plates, refilled coffee cups and smiled privately when Malia wriggled out of Jane's grasp and toddled to Tom, who was in conversation with Peggy.

The gesture looked so natural, it couldn't have been better if she'd staged it.

Her father sat on Tom's other side, also involved in their conversation while he dandled Garrett on his knee.

Her mother watched him with a pleased smile. Jane studied him with a kind of lambent lust. Amy's older sister had always been so controlled, so cool, that Amy had always wondered if there was any warmth inside her. She'd rarely exhibited it.

And the fact that she'd chosen to love a man who, despite a law firm partnership three years out of law school, had all the animation of a mannequin tended to confirm that she didn't.

But now Amy wondered. Had Jane secretly harbored a longing all this time for a big-shouldered man in a T-shirt?

And Peggy, who'd starred opposite Christian Slater, Alec Baldwin and Ethan Brennan, seemed fascinated with him.

Amy thought she might burst with a sense of success. In a couple of days, when they were all back home, she would write them and confess everything, absolving Tom of all responsibility. It was the coward's way out without a doubt, but she was simply enjoying these few hours too much to give them up.

Later, when Tom was finished with the barn and gone, and she was alone again with other people's children, she would live on the memory of this morning and the fact that for several hours she'd been Rich Amy. Really Rich Amy.

Then her mother dropped the bomb.

"Well, my goodness!" She fluttered slim-fingered hands, jewels glittering on each ring finger and pinkie. "In all the excitement, we forgot to tell you what we're doing here!"

"I thought it was just your every few years' visit," Amy said, a little sense of foreboding creeping into her flush of success.

"Peggy just finished doing a special show for Isaac Mizrahi and called to say she was coming home with an announcement!"

Amy kept smiling. "And that was?" She turned to Peggy, expecting her to explain, but she seemed not to be following the conversation. There was a pleat between her eyebrows as she watched the babies.

Sabina leaned toward Amy, flushed with excitement. "First of all, she's going to be in a movie with Brad Pitt!"

Amy reacted with appropriate astonishment. It was remarkable, when she thought about it. Her sister in a movie opposite one of the moment's prime sex symbols. But then Peggy had always been remarkable.

"Congratulations!" Amy said. "That's wonderful, Peggy."

Peggy seemed to bring the conversation back into focus. She smiled. "Thank you."

"It starts filming next week," her mother went on, "so she has to fly to Hawaii on Monday. And…" There was a sort of "da-da!" quality to her mother's pause. "She's getting married on Sunday! To Ethan Brennan! Isn't that so exciting! The hottest box-office draw in the last three years and our Peggy got him!"

Jane smiled. At least that was how Amy interpreted the little quirk of her bottom lip. "We're so happy for her," Jane said in a tone more suited to "and there were no survivors."

"Anyway…" her mother went on, letting Chelsea go when she started to fuss. The baby ran to Amy, who lifted her into her lap. "We called Jane and Beau's office and arranged to meet them at Logan Airport so we could charter a plane, come west and pick you up, then fly on to Seattle where Ethan's family is. Then Ethan's off to Toronto for filming while Peggy goes to Hawaii." She bobbed her elegant golden blond bun from side to side in a we-do-what-we-must gesture. "Gstaad would have been a more romantic setting, but *c'est la guerre.*"

Amy knew she'd heard all the facts, but all she could focus on at the moment was "pick you up, then fly on to Seattle."

"So." Nelson Brown took the plastic truck Garrett offered him. "You're not as footloose as we'd imagined. Can you come?"

Thank God, Amy thought instantly. An out.

"I'm so happy for you, Peggy," she said, reaching

out to touch her sister's hand. Then she gestured around the room to the three babies, now moving in three different directions. "But it isn't very easy for us to just pick up and..."

"Amy," Peggy said, holding on to her hand as she tried to withdraw it. "You've got to come. Please." There was something desperate in her eyes. Amy focused on it, certain she must be mistaken. Peggy had never needed her for anything, even as a child. And when they'd all grown up, she'd been openly scornful of Amy's little dreams.

"Darling, you can't deprive us of an opportunity to get to know our new son-in-law and grandbabies." Her mother looked severe. "Particularly considering we're being very civilized about the fact that you didn't even tell us about them."

She had her there. "But Tom has work...." she argued futilely, now even afraid to look in Tom's direction.

"Your mother's right," her father said. "You owe us that much."

It was on the tip of Amy's tongue to tell him that she didn't owe them anything, that all the time she and her sisters were growing up, the only accomplishments their parents had appreciated in their children had been Jane's scholastic ability and Peggy's beauty.

Amy's talents were making friends and being happy even when the situation didn't warrant it. But those accomplishments had been far too small to deserve their notice. And when she'd blossomed like a weed rather than a rose, tall and sturdy and plain, she'd become Poor Amy.

But Amy tried to suppress that whole line of thinking. In her child-care experience, she was learning that many people were gifted parents and as many were not. But what seemed common to most of them was that they did their best in a job that was demanding, relentless and terrifying.

Also—it was hard to fault them for their behavior when hers this morning was reprehensible. And she couldn't even think about trying to straighten it out now because then she would ruin Peggy's wedding. So she just had to go with it. She couldn't in all conscience be sanctimonious with them.

Peggy squeezed her hand again. "Please, Amy."

Amy squeezed back, at a loss to explain her younger sister's behavior. Her need seemed very genuine.

Amy turned to her parents. "Would you mind if Tom and I talk it over for a few minutes?" She stood and reached for Tom's hand, praying he wouldn't ignore it, or worse yet, slap it away and spill the truth.

"Of course not," her mother said. "Go ahead. We'll watch the babies. And Daddy and I are picking up all expenses, so that's something to figure into your considerations."

Tom caught her hand, but he did not allow her to lead him out, he led her, and at a pace that had her airborne by the time they reached her bedroom.

He pushed her in before him and leaned back against the door like a sentry after closing it.

"Tell me again," he challenged her, folding his arms, "how this shouldn't be too hard, how it'll only take two hours then they'll all disperse back to their—"

She rolled her eyes impatiently. "All right!" she shouted in a whisper. "I'm sorry! Every other time we've come together since my high school graduation, it's been for a few hours at a time. Except for Jane's wedding, and that was just one day long and there were hundreds of other people there.''

She fell onto the edge of the bed with a groan. ''Frankly, I have no idea what to do. If I tell them the truth, I ruin Peggy's wedding, and for some reason she seems so...I don't know...insecure, or something. She clung to my hand. She's never done that.''

She looked at him for understanding. He didn't seem willing to offer it. So she continued to explain.

''If we do go with them, we've got two major, *major* strikes against us.''

''Only two?''

She ignored his sarcasm and went on. ''We're traveling with three two-year-olds. And I really don't see us being able to pull off being married.''

''So you want to tell them?''

''No.''

''Then we'll have to pull it off.''

Amy was surprised to hear him concede that. She was sure it was the only way to go, but it amazed her that he was willing to consider it.

''Do you think you can? I mean, you'll actually have to talk to me as though I'm there,'' she said. ''Not like you're dealing with a hologram or a personal representative.''

She surprised herself with that remark. She hadn't realized she'd been sitting on that resentment until she blurted it out.

Tom, too, focused on her eyes as though there'd been a revelation in that little outburst.

''You act like a hologram,'' he retorted quietly, ''or as though you've sent in a stand-in. You say the words, you do the actions, but there's nothing behind it, nothing inside.''

She stood up angrily. "You didn't behave as though you felt that way the night of the party."

"That's because you were you the night of the party," he retorted. "It was when I suggested you leave your work to spend a little time with me that you suddenly sent in a double."

"You don't understand."

"No, I don't. Just like when I had to leave two years ago, you didn't understand. Apparently ours isn't a marriage made in heaven, despite our three little angels." He straightened away from the door and took hold of the knob. "Let's just do this. I can make it through Sunday night if you can. And try to look happier about it, or we're not going to fool anybody."

"Yeah, right," she said grimly, coming to the door, waiting for him to open it. "Like your approach to this would inspire love and joy in a woman."

"Well." He caught her arm and pulled her to him. "Let's see what I can do about that."

He lowered his head and opened his mouth over hers, giving her a kiss that swiftly cleared her mind of thought. He caught one hand in her hair and lowered the other to her hip and held her against him with it, stroking her, reminding her of all they'd had together that night, and all she'd missed since.

Then he raised his head and looked into her eyes. She knew they had to reflect the instant rush of desire that had raced through her.

He grinned with arrogant satisfaction. "That's better. Now, put a little soul into your performance, Amy. You can't send in a double for this one." He opened the door and pushed her through it.

THEY WERE IN SEATTLE for lunch.

GARRETT: The airplane was cool! I'm going to pilot a

ship to Mars, you know. And when I'm done doing that, I'm going to be president. Hey, look. There's a flying saucer on a stick.

MALIA: Jerk! That's the Space Needle. I think our hotel's around here someplace. We're going to be in a wedding! I heard that lady who thinks she's our grandma talking, and she says she's going to buy us matching outfits!

GARRETT: Oh, no! I'm not wearing an *outfit*. Those things end up having doodads all over them and I'll look like a girl. Nothing doing!

CHELSEA: Astronauts wear outfits. It's the same thing. It's just that this is a wedding. You'll end up looking very handsome.

GARRETT: You think so?

CHELSEA: Of course. How could you be anything else?

GARRETT: All right, then.

MALIA: Good one, Chelsea.

CHELSEA: I try.

SABINA HAD CALLED AHEAD to book the bridal suite of the Seattle Roxbury Arms.

A bellhop led them to the top floor and into an enormous living area filled with sofas and chairs and a large dining table. A small kitchen was set to one side and a glorious view of the city was visible through the large window on the other.

"The cribs are in this room," the bellhop said, leading Tom and Amy into the largest of the four rooms that radiated off the living area like spokes.

It was huge. Amy didn't know where they'd found three matching cribs, but they had, and they were arranged in a row at the foot of the room.

On the other end was a king-size bed and two end tables with stained glass reading lamps. A little sofa stood under a window that looked onto the city from another angle.

"The hotel has a full day-care facility if you need it," the bellhop said as Tom tipped him. The babies, set on their feet, took off in all directions. "Press 11 on the telephone. Thank you, sir."

Amy began pulling off the babies' coats and Tom squatted down to help her.

Sabina carried in a box of toys they'd brought along. "I guess the most efficient thing to do," she said, dusting off her hands, "is to have lunch, then we'll leave the men behind to watch the babies while we get our dresses. Ethan's parents will be meeting us in the restaurant for dinner at about the same time Ethan, himself, arrives from London where *he's* been filming. Don't you love it?"

Amy ignored that question because she had one of her own. "Dresses? But I brought..."

Her mother was shaking her head. "Just because we're doing this quickly is no reason not to do it right. And Ethan's parents and friends will be here. You and Jane will have matching dresses, and I'll be a stunning mother of the bride." She clasped her hands together in a near-swoon of anticipation. "Peggy's going to wear a dress she modeled for Isaac Mizrahi!"

Great, Amy thought. She and Jane in matching dresses, so everyone could see how delicate and chic Jane looked in hers, and how robust and out of place Amy appeared in the same thing.

Sabina smiled at Tom. "You brought along a suit?"

Amy had thought about that when they'd taken a precious hour to pack while her mother walked around the living room like a field marshal checking assault plans. Because of the nature of child care, Amy had enough changes of baby clothes on hand to make her fabrication appear real, but when it came to Tom, he had only the clothes on his back. She could not have explained away his going home and returning with a suitcase, so they'd opted to buy him a few things when they arrived.

"I don't own one," he lied with a charming smile. "But I saw a clothing store in the lobby. I'll find something."

Sabina seemed more intrigued than shocked that a man could live his life without a suit. "You charge it to the room and we'll take care of it." She patted Tom's cheek. "I'm sure none of Ethan's actor friends could be any more handsome than you are."

"Don't let it go to your head," Amy said to Tom under her breath as her mother left the room. She took something out of Garrett's hand, and discovered to her horror that it was a knob. "Oh, no. What is this from?" GARRETT: Cool, huh? Right over there. That thing with the drawers against the wall. It just came right off. Don't you like it?

"Don't panic," Tom said, taking it from her and going to the dresser. "It screws right back in. No, Garrett.

We have to put it back.''

GARRETT: But it's mine! I found it and gave it to Amy! No! Give it back!

Tom pulled the screaming toddler into his arms, handed him back the drawer pull, then guided his hand into screwing it back in place.

Garrett abruptly stopped screaming, distracted by the small action. He had to unscrew it and replace it several more times. Tom stood by patiently, and Amy thought, not for the first time, how good he was with the babies. She shouldn't be surprised of course, he'd always been a big part of Eddy's and Pete's lives.

He grinned at Amy over his shoulder.

''Wait till I tell Nate the kid's showing signs of being a carpenter rather than a doctor,'' he said.

She smiled, sharing the joke with him. For a brief moment, it was sweet to share something, then Malia and Chelsea got into a tug-of-war over a roll of toilet paper Chelsea found in the bathroom, and Amy lost the moment's peace.

''YOU'RE GOING TO LEAVE *three* babies with Beau and me?'' Amy's father asked in obvious concern over lunch. Three high chairs were distributed among the six adults seated around the coffee shop's largest table. Other diners were staring at Peggy. She was seldom recognized as an actress or a runway model, but was always noticed for her spectacular beauty.

''Tom will be in the men's shop right here in the lobby,'' Sabina said calmly, ''and he'll be right back when he's finished. Won't you, dear?''

"I have briefs to review," Beau said. There was real panic in his serious hazel eyes.

"Oh, for heaven's sake!" Jane snapped at him. "You're an uncle! You can put work aside long enough to get acquainted with your nieces and nephew."

Everyone except Tom turned in surprise at Jane's uncharacteristic outburst.

Jane shifted uncomfortably and stabbed at a slice of sautéed vegetable with her fork. "I asked him not to bring work," she offered querulously by way of explanation.

"Darling," Sabina said quietly, leaning toward her. "We're in public."

Jane scraped her chair back, slapped her napkin down and said at the top of her voice, "I don't care if we're on the stage at Carnegie Hall! He works eighty hours a week and spends twenty of the other forty in the law library! The rest of the time I get to watch him sleep! I *asked* him not to bring work with him...."

Amy, seated beside Jane, caught her hand. She wasn't sure what her intentions were, but touch often worked with children who were too upset to be coherent.

Jane stopped her tirade and looked down at Amy in complete surprise. She glanced around at the other diners who'd stopped eating to stare at her, and fell into her chair with a sigh.

Embarrassed, Sabina fanned herself with a tent card from the middle of the table that advertised hors d'oeuvres.

Nelson smiled sympathetically at Jane while patting Sabina's shoulder. "Whatever's bothering you, baby," he said gently, "it'll be all right. Don't you worry."

Jane looked into Amy's eyes, and Amy saw there the same grimness she'd always felt when her father repeated his favorite platitude. It was the code that governed his life. *Don't worry.* However, he failed to back up that directive with any effort to relieve the source of concern.

Amy had learned early on that he would always love his daughters, but he was incapable of taking charge of anything to help them. Representatives had always run his business, and their mother had always run their home. All he'd ever had to do was tell everyone not to worry.

Amy rubbed gently up and down Jane's spine. Jane turned to her with another look of surprise and a whispered "thank you."

Chapter Eleven

Amy tried to zip herself into the sophisticated rose taffeta gown Peggy and Sabina had decided would look wonderful in the hotel's white-and-silver garden room where the wedding would take place.

"You'll look like a pair of roses," Sabina said. "A tea rose..." She smiled at small, slender Jane who didn't seem to be paying attention to business at all. "And a...a cabbage rose," she added for Amy after a panicky hesitation. "Those *must* have a more romantic name."

Amy had to laugh. "A cabbage by any other name..." she said, and shouldering the dress, headed off toward the dressing rooms while Peggy and Sabina moved on to mother-of-the-bride dresses.

Even a long-stemmed rose, she thought wryly, wouldn't be able to reach this zipper.

"Amy?"

The voice was small and sounded exasperated. It belonged to Jane in the next dressing room.

"Yes?" Amy replied.

"Could you come and help me?"

For a moment, Amy stood transfixed. That was a first.

Controlled, self-sufficient Jane was asking the cabbage rose for help?

Amy left her dressing room and rapped lightly on the louvered doors of Jane's.

Jane pulled it open and turned back to the mirror quickly, but not before Amy saw a tear well out of brimming blue eyes.

Amy tugged gently down on the fabric at the base of the zipper and drew the tab up over a delicate, crenulated spinal column. "Janie, are you all right?" she asked, taking a step to the side to look at her sister's reflection in the mirror.

The vivid color of the dress lent drama to her fine features and color to her milky complexion. She looked beautiful...and very sad.

Jane moved to get behind Amy and returned the favor, pulling up her zipper. "You look very beautiful," she said, stepping out from behind her so that they were both reflected in the mirror.

Amy studied the two images and felt a moment's debilitating shock. Jane was as beautiful as Peggy, but her petite proportions made her look like a porcelain doll, delicate and precious.

But she, Amy, looked...beautiful, too. She studied the face looking back at her and wondered what it was that had changed.

Feature by feature, she was far less dramatic in appearance, but she'd learned over the last few years to make the most of her silver-blond hair and gray eyes. And her hard work and determination showed, defining the contours of her mouth and chin.

Perhaps it was Kids & Co. She'd done it all on her own, it was successful, and it had all the promise of being even more so. If that was what she wanted. Maybe success affected looks.

Then she thought about Tom, and watched something subtle change in her expression.

It was pain, she thought wryly. Suffering. Loving Tom had put her through the proverbial mill. Then she felt a smile bubble up inside her and she accepted that she'd gotten as much love and laughter from him as distress. It was just that they weren't sure how to put it all together.

Her expression changed again, and for a moment, there was a strong family resemblance between herself and Jane. It was in the grimness of the set of the mouth, the melancholy in the eyes. Her problem, she knew, was that she felt something precious slipping away from her and didn't know how to hold on to it.

Was Jane's problem the same?

"Are you and Beau having...trouble?" she asked, then added quickly, "I know it's none of my business, and you don't have to answer me if you don't want to. I just hate to see you so...upset."

Jane sniffed and looked at Amy's reflection. "I can see that you do," she said, seeming genuinely puzzled. "I saw that in you at the restaurant. But I thought you never liked me."

Amy was at a loss for a moment, feeling as though the subject of sisterly affection was just too big for the confines of the dressing room. "Of course I like you. You're my sister."

"Yeah." Jane fussed with the flared sleeve distractedly. "But this isn't exactly the 'Brady Bunch,' is it? I mean, we don't support one another, we compete." She sighed and pulled at the band that held her platinum hair in a tight knot. "Mom wants us to be perfect, and

Dad wants us not to worry—so he won't have to. They don't care if you have a problem, as long as you don't show it.''

Amy experienced both relief and panic. Jane felt all the same things she felt—only Amy had suppressed them so long, she wasn't sure she wanted to deal with them now. So, she tried to sidestep to Jane's issues.

"So you *do* have a problem?"

Jane combed her hair with her fingers as another tear slid down her cheek. "I think it's over between Beau and me. He does nothing but work. I mean, I married him because he was ambitious, but this is ridiculous. I think he uses it as a way of staying away from me."

"Why would he want to do that?" Amy asked logically. "You're beautiful and brilliant. You have everything."

"I'm also afraid of everything," Jane said with a sigh. And that little gesture seemed to open something inside her that she must have kept closed for a long time. Her tears began to fall more freely, and her bottom lip quivered. "I'd be terrified of a man like your Tom."

Amy blinked. Tom and terror were an impossible equation. Tom and murder—maybe.

"Whatever for?"

Jane burst into sobs. "Because all I've ever gotten from Beau is gentle, respectful, he-following-my-lead kind of sex, and I'm sick of it! He *must* hate me—or feel nothing when he touches me, which is even worse!" She wept brokenheartedly.

Amy drew her into her arms and felt as though the real world had disintegrated and she was living in some mirror world inhabited by the same people, but with personalities she no longer recognized.

"Beau's just not very…animated. In fact, I remember

when you called to tell me you were getting married, you said that you loved him because he was always temperate. He didn't run hot or cold.''

Jane tightened her grip on her as she continued to weep. ''God. I don't know what's happening to me. It isn't like me to whine and be dissatisfied.'' Amy found a box of tissue on a shelf and handed her one. ''Thank you. I used to be able to be the perfect doll with a brain that Mom created, but...I don't know. Maybe I'm getting a little older. Maybe my hormones are surging. But...''

She drew away from Amy and made an expressive gesture with her hands and the fluttering tissue. ''I *want* stuff. I want kisses that mean something, I want sex that's out of control, I want Beau to call me from the office and tell me that he has lascivious plans for me when he comes home. I want to be more important to him than his work.''

She pressed the tissue to her nose and sobbed again. When she stopped, she blurted, her voice frail, ''I want a baby!'' Then she began to sob anew.

Amy pushed her gently onto the seat built into the dressing room wall.

''*I* want you to take deep breaths,'' she said, stroking her sister's hair. ''And I don't want you to say a word until you stop choking. You stay right here. I have a bottle of water in my purse.''

Amy retrieved the bottle, uncapped it and gave it to Jane, playing for time. How did one advise a sister who felt as though her marriage was on the rocks because she was comparing it to hers—which really didn't exist?

''Beau won't hear of it,'' Jane said finally, her voice quieter, her breathing more normal, though tears continued to flow. "He says we have to get the house on Back Bay before we have a baby."

"Because there'll be too many expenses afterward?"

Jane balled the tissue into her fist and sniffed. "I guess. I don't know."

"You didn't ask?" Amy leaned against the opposite wall and watched Jane shake her head. "Have you told him how you feel about…sex being unsatisfactory?"

Jane shook her head again. "Should I have to? I mean, if sex wasn't satisfying for you, don't you think Tom would know it? Do you think he'd even let it happen?"

Amy remembered vividly his consummate care and attention to her every gasp and sigh the night he'd made love to her. Then she pushed that thought from her mind before she became overloaded with her own concerns and couldn't focus on Jane's. "We're all different, Janie. I think before you chuck it all, you should sit him down, tell him what you're feeling, and make him tell you why he's working late and why he doesn't want a baby. After watching him react to the news that he and Dad were going to have to watch the babies this afternoon, I'd say he was afraid of them. But I think that's pretty common, and that fear is usually dismissed by spending a little time with one."

Jane sniffed again, seemed to consider her advice, then rose slowly to her feet and studied her with something Amy couldn't remember ever seeing on her face before—affection.

"Thank you, Amy," Jane said. She drew a breath and she seemed to grow an inch, Amy thought. "I don't know that any of that will work, but…I've felt so alone in all this. But I don't feel that anymore." She smiled with a little spark of sincere joy. "I never thought of you as being on my side."

"I didn't know you wanted me there."

"When I was trying to be Mom's perfect showpiece, I was such a snot. I think I felt like you didn't have a chance," she said, the brutal honesty tempered with a self-deprecating smile. "What I never saw was that Peggy and I were clones. You were an original."

Amy laughed. "Only because I was too large and too klutzy to be a clone. I really wanted to be. I just didn't have what it took. And I hated myself and resented all of you because of it for a long time."

"Until Tom?"

Amy thought about that. It was Tom's leaving that had made her get herself together. And his coming back that had left her in a shambles.

She was saved from having to answer when the sound of Peggy's and Sabina's voices drifted into the dressing rooms area.

"I hope this dress is as perfect as it appears on the hanger," Sabina was saying. "The diagonal cut on the bodice sort of reflects the cut of your dress, don't you think?"

"It's a pretty dress, Mom." Peggy sounded weary. "You try it on. I'll see how Amy and Jane are doing. Guys?"

"Right here." Amy and Jane moved out into the common area and the three-way mirror. Peggy looked into Jane's still pink-and-puffy face and glanced at Amy. "What's wrong?"

"Man trouble," Jane said, quickly dismissing her sister's question while she turned in front of the mirror. "Nothing that's going to spoil your wedding. What do you think? Do we look great?"

Jane and Amy posed, did a few theatrical turns, and Peggy laughed. It occurred to Amy that she looked as though the laugh was a relief, as though it had to struggle out of her past some great obstruction.

She didn't look like a happy bride at all.

"You look wonderful," she said, and came to put a hand on each of them. Then she said in mild surprise, "I've missed you."

Jane hugged her, then reached out to pull Amy into their embrace. Amy, feeling as though she was moving deeper and deeper into that mirror world, let them enfold her. But the sting of tears in her eyes was very real.

AMY WAS SO HAPPY to see Tom and the babies again. She even went into his arms, not because she thought it would make their relationship look authentic, but because...well, she wasn't sure. Her first thought was that he provided balance in her life, but he didn't really. He'd turned it upside down. Maybe it was just that he seemed so sane and uncomplicated when compared with her family.

She excused herself from the rest of the group and led him into their room.

"How are the kids?" she asked, clinging to him.

"Fine," he replied. "Napping. Rough day?"

"Just...complicated. Maybe I'll take a nap myself."

He patted her back, and she thought the gesture had the suggestion of apology. "No time," he said. "Ethan called. He's here, and he and his family are meeting us in the dining room in half an hour."

She groaned and leaned her head against his shoulder with a thunk. "I don't know why I let you talk me into this trip," she teased.

"It was because you always do what I ask," he replied in the same tone.

"Why don't you ask me to go home?" she suggested, still leaning on him.

"Now?" he asked, laughter in his voice. "After we've defrauded your family and kidnapped three babies? We're probably just getting to the good part."

She closed her eyes and sighed. "Well. As long as there's going to be a good part."

He was quiet, and she lifted her face to look at him, wondering what had squelched the playful mood, and encountered the look Jane admitted to being afraid of. It was hot and demanding and deliciously dangerous.

But Amy had not an instant's trepidation. She stretched up as he leaned down and their lips fused in a kiss that seemed to be about reunion, resurgence, regeneration.

His hands moved over her as hers explored him, and she thought it couldn't make sense to feel this passionately about someone with whom she knew she had no future. Unless it was that pretending they shared a future made it real enough to confuse their libidos.

A rap on the door broke the kiss but left them clinging to each other.

"We're due in the dining room in twenty-five minutes!" Sabina called cheerfully through the door. "Do try to look nice. Ethan's parents will be there. His dad's a surgeon," she added as an aside, "and Ethan's costar from 'Cleveland Cops' is going to be his best man. He's here, too."

TOM DISLIKED Ethan Brennan on sight. He had no justification for it, except a gut feeling that would be difficult to explain to anyone else. But he'd gone into burning buildings with many men, and there were those you trusted, and those you didn't.

It was as simple as that.

Brennan was tall and muscular, and though hotel security had to push back hordes of young people when he and his friend left the limo for the hotel, Tom could honestly say he'd never even seen a photo of him. Or if he had, it hadn't meant much because he wasn't into popular movies.

He had blond hair tied back in a short ponytail and wore a wrinkled jacket over a silk shirt and a pair of jeans. His appearance made Tom wonder what the fuss had been about "looking nice."

His friend, Bill Channing, was of similar height and build, but his hair was dark and buzz cut. According to Sabina, they'd just made some kind of buddy movie together, and they appeared to have held on to the bigger-than-life swagger probably common to men who have the lines written for them and stunt-doubles to take their risks.

But they were polite and affable, and Tom thought the weird weekend might just have given him a skewed outlook on everything.

Amy included. He wanted to kill Channing when he was introduced to Amy and brought her hand to his lips. But she yanked her hand away from him when he held it too long. Channing blinked at her, as though unable to believe his attentions were being scorned, and Tom was satisfied.

Beau came to stand beside him. They'd watched a 49ers game together while Nelson slept and the babies climbed all over them. Despite Beau's appearance of having a frozen core, Tom had concluded that he was all right.

"Big stuff," Beau said.

"So it seems."

Brennan pulled Peggy to him and security cleared their path through the hotel and into the dining room. Amy's family closed ranks behind them.

Tom was surprised that Brennan's parents were already seated at the large table. "Can't stand that crowd and fuss," the senior Brennan said, pulling out Sabina's chair. "And we had all the dinner rolls to ourselves. Julian Brennan. My wife, Dora."

Introductions were made all over again, and Tom found Amy studying Brennan over her menu as conversation buzzed around the table. He gathered from the set of her jaw that she didn't like him, either.

And he was beginning to see what her problem was with her parents—why she had the overwhelming need to prove something to herself and to them. They seemed to credit all their daughters only with how they looked, what they had, and what they'd achieved. There was none of the love for love's sake that abounded in his family. No unconditional devotion just because you were you.

No wonder she didn't understand him when he told her that all he wanted was her. She'd never been valued that way before. He needed a new tack.

MALIA: Hi! How was Ethan Brennan? Was he as gorgeous as he is in the movies? Did you mention my name? Tell him I'm available to do location work? Eddy says I'm cute enough to do commercials, but I think I'd prefer film.

CHELSEA: Hi! The lady from the hotel day care was very nice, but we thought it would be rude to be asleep when you came home 'cause we thought you'd want to tell us all about it! Did you bring back any leftovers?

GARRETT: About those outfits that grandma-person bought. I'm not wearing mine. Girls can wear little animals and flowers, but I'm into plaids and denim. And this hotel day-care lady tried to give me milk in a bottle! I tried to tell her I'm using a cup, but I guess we don't speak the same language. Could I have some now, please?

Amy and Tom were greeted by a frazzled sitter when the group arrived home. Everyone else said their goodnights and drifted off to their rooms, apparently reluctant to deal with three wide-awake two-year-olds at one in the morning. Amy could certainly understand.

And she was the one pretending to be the mom.

She left Tom in charge and went to the kitchen to fill Chelsea's and Malia's bottles and Garrett's two-handled cup with milk.

She came back to the bedroom to find the three tumbling on the mattress under Tom's supervision amid uproarious giggling. He looked up from their antics as she returned, and she saw him smiling with the infectious quality of their laughter.

It occurred to her that that ability was probably rare in a man at that hour.

Then Malia, a little more exuberant than the other two, tumbled a little too close to the edge. But good reflexes and a long reach allowed him to boost her back toward the middle of the bed.

They were having such a good time, Amy feared that relaxing them with bottles would be hopeless, at least for a while, but Chelsea came for hers greedily and settled down immediately into the crook of Amy's arm.

Amy leaned back against the head of the bed with a sigh while Tom tried to lure Malia to him with her bottle. But she was still too rambunctious. Garrett, however, was happy to take his cup.

Tom had pulled off his shoes and lay propped on an elbow across the foot of the bed so that Garrett could lean against him, but so that he could still guide Malia's tumbles.

"I didn't like him," Amy said, the niggle of worry that had bothered her throughout the evening coming forward with insistence.

Tom smoothed Garrett's hair. "I know. I didn't, either. But he's Peggy's choice."

Amy leaned her head back. "I can't help but wonder why."

"What do you mean? Didn't his mother say *People* magazine just voted him second sexiest man alive, or something?"

She made a face and rolled her eyes. "He might have something that comes across on the screen, but in person he seems so…disconnected or something. I got the feeling he found us all very boring and was wishing he was somewhere else." She pulled a corner of the bedspread up over Chelsea as the toddler's eyes began to close. "And I don't like the way he kisses Peggy."

Tom arched an eyebrow at that. "But apparently she does."

Amy made another face that made him smile. It involved a wrinkled nose and a curious downward twist to her mouth he guessed meant revulsion. "First of all, I don't think it's cool to kiss open-mouthed at the table or in front of your fiancée's family. And secondly, though he has all the mechanics of kissing down, he has none of the style.''

"Really?"

"Yes." She was distracted now, her eyes unfocused as she apparently thought back on the scene. "He could learn a lot from you."

Then she seemed to realize what she'd said, and she pretended absorption in Chelsea. He was sure she was going to retract the statement, or at least qualify it. But she didn't. After a moment she relaxed and gave him a small smile.

"Don't look so surprised," she said, smoothing Chelsea's bald head. "You know you're a good kisser."

He put a hand to his heart. "But I'm honored to know you think so, too. Whoa!" That same hand reached out just in time to catch Malia as she tumbled dangerously close to Garrett's face. He pinned her in the crook of the arm on which he supported himself and offered her the bottle again. "If we don't get her to sleep, we're going to look pretty rough for the wedding."

MALIA: Come on! It's still early! People come to Seattle for the nightlife—I heard it on TV. I don't want...oh, all right. But what a pair of rubes you two turned out to be.

Malia took her bottle and was soon rubbing her eyes and resisting their gradual drift closed.

Tom looked down at Garrett just in time to catch the cup as his little hand went slack around the handle. He transferred it to the hand that held Malia. Garrett's eyes popped open, but Tom pushed him gently down to the mattress and rubbed his back. He was back to sleep in a moment. Malia began to snore.

"I suppose we don't dare move," Tom said quietly, "or everyone's going to wake up again."

Amy nodded. "Let's just give them a few minutes." Her eyes went from baby to baby in that perpetual sweep he'd noticed at home. But this time, two of the babies were all entangled with him, so he received that watchful, analytical glance, as well.

He thought he saw something wistful in it. "What are you thinking?" he asked softly.

She sighed and gently pulled the bottle from Chelsea's little pursed lips. They continued to make a perfect circle, even after the bottle was removed.

"I was thinking that this is nice," she said. Her voice had a dreamy quality.

"What? Being awake at—" he checked his watch "—1:45 a.m.?"

"The peace," she corrected him with a scolding glance. Then she gave him a look that might have buckled his knees had he been upright. It was filled with need and confusion—and gratitude. "Did I ever thank you for agreeing to do this?"

"I figured it was implied," he answered.

"You should know it's appreciated. Thank you."

"You're welcome."

"Jane wants a baby." He was beginning to recognize a sudden shift in topic as her modus operandi when she was upset.

He grinned. "Well, we've got three."

She gave him that look again that was half laughter, half reprimand. "She wants to get pregnant. But she thinks her marriage is over."

"Why?"

"Because Beau spends most of his time at work."

"He's buying a house in some exclusive area of Boston."

Her eyes widened in surprise. "Back Bay. How do you know that?"

"He told me," Tom replied in a whisper as Garrett shifted position.

"I thought guys didn't have those kinds of discussions. Particularly with strangers."

He didn't understand the problem. "About houses?"

"About plans. Dreams."

"Well, it's a fact, not a dream, and when you've spent an entire afternoon side by side in combat with three babies, you're no longer strangers."

"Didn't my father help?"

"No. He told us not to worry, that the babies would be fine. Then he took a nap."

Amy frowned apologetically. "How did you find time to buy clothes?"

"I didn't want to leave Beau alone with all three, so I brought the girls with me, and a couple of the clerks helped keep an eye on them while I bought a suit. When we got back, Beau was doing fine with Garrett. I think he kind of got into it. He's really all right."

Amy gingerly swung her legs over the side of the bed and got to her feet without waking Chelsea. She put her into the crib, covered her and returned to the bed to scoop Garrett into her arms.

He protested sleepily, but she put him to her shoulder and he fell asleep again. When she eased him into the second crib, he didn't stir.

Tom held Malia to him and stood. She groaned, made a face, rubbed her eyes and fussed when he placed her in the crib. But he gave her her pacifier and patted her back, and she was asleep in a minute.

He and Amy collapsed against each other in congratulations. Then she went into the bathroom and he stripped down to T-shirt and briefs and climbed into bed.

She was back in a minute in a cotton nightgown and climbed in beside him, leaving a body's space between them.

He started to turn away from her, intent on diminishing the agony he knew was in store for him over the next few hours as they lay side by side without touching.

But she caught his shoulder and turned him toward her, pulling the blankets up over both their heads. For a blissful instant, he thought she was inviting him into her arms—but she wanted only to talk.

"What do you mean, the house is a fact?" she whispered under the acoustical confidence of the blankets.

He struggled for equilibrium in the wake of disappointment. "What house?"

She clicked her tongue. "The house you and Beau talked about."

"I *mean* that he's bought it."

"Why didn't he tell Jane?"

"Amy, how would I know that?"

"Well, you said you had a chummy chat."

"About a house, not about why he can't confide in his wife. Now, I'm sure you'll manage to look beautiful in the morning, anyway, but I spent all afternoon with the kids while you were shopping, and spent most of dinner listening to your mom and Mrs. Brennan try to out-name-drop each other. I'm beat."

He couldn't see her in the undercover darkness, but he got a distinct sense of hurt feelings.

"Of course," she whispered. "Good night." And she turned over, folding the blankets back again.

He felt a clutch of guilt and exasperation. "Amy," he said, and caught her shoulder, trying to turn her toward him. "I didn't mean to bark at you."

She resisted his efforts and kept her back to him. "It's all right," she whispered, but he could hear a sob in her voice. "I'm fine. Go to sleep."

It would be safer to do that, he knew, but his conscience wouldn't let him. He forced an arm under her and turned her bodily toward him, a little surprised but pleased when she offered no resistance.

"Is something bothering you," he asked quietly, and with amusement, "about your sister's marriage problems? I mean, we *are* lying, but your family thinks we're the ideal couple and that our babies are miracles of genetic engineering. I thought you'd be happy to have one up on her?"

He was further surprised when she dissolved into tears against him. He pulled the blankets up over their heads again to muffle the sound. In their little cocoon of woven cotton he simply held her and waited out the storm, blotting out all thought of how her softness felt against him, trying to ignore all awareness of her knee riding up and down his leg in distress.

"That's not my priority anymore," she admitted in a choked whisper as she tried to catch her breath. "We were helping each other into the dresses this afternoon in this teeny little dressing room and she started to cry."

She wept a little more, and she wasn't sure if it was in sympathy for her sister or for herself.

He continued to hold her close, ignoring the ravages to his own nervous system.

"She told me that they have dull sex," she went on,

her arm hooking unconsciously over his waist, wedging her body even closer to his and unconsciously assuring him that if the opportunity arose for *them* to have sex, it would not be dull. "And that she feels the same way about our family that I've always felt. Like she'd be left out in a minute if she wasn't beautiful and perfect. The only difference is that she was able to be, so she got stuck in it longer than I did."

Tom kissed her cheek in comfort. His family was so loving and supportive no matter how difficult or stupid or wrong you were that it hurt to imagine a young and vulnerable Amy without that kind of love.

"And all that time, she thought I didn't like her and didn't care about her...." She turned her face into his throat and added in a strained voice, "And I was thinking the same about her. So when we maybe could have helped each other, we were...I guess...busy saving ourselves."

She raised her head and looked down into his eyes. Her own were tear-filled and unhappy. "Isn't that awful?"

He brushed her hair back and tucked it behind her ear. "It is. But your mom's too superficial and your dad's too disconnected for it to be different. You didn't do anything wrong. And if you and Jane have started talking about it, you can probably reestablish a relationship."

"Yeah." She settled into his shoulder, that arm hooking chummily around him again. "I wish I could get Peggy to tell me what's wrong."

"You mean, besides the boyfriend?"

"I don't think she loves him. I don't think she even likes him."

"Then, why would she be marrying him? She certainly doesn't need the money or the publicity."

Amy nuzzled into him with a deep sigh. "I have no idea. And I'm too tired to think straight. But I'm glad you're here, Tom. I'm really glad you're here."

He closed his eyes and gritted his teeth as she threw a leg over him. "Yeah," he said, pulling the blankets down and taking a gulp of air. "Me, too."

Chapter Twelve

MALIA: Wow! Do we look great, or what? I understand the press will be here! Chelsea, this could be our chance to get a gig like the Olson twins.

CHELSEA: Lia, are you forgetting that we aren't *really* related? We're pretending to be triplets, but we don't look anything alike. I can't believe these people haven't noticed.

MALIA: We don't have to look alike. All we have to do is be cute and charming. We can do it. Well, I can do it.

GARRETT: Yeah, well you're doing it without me. I told you before this outfit was going to make me look like a girl, and I was right.

CHELSEA: Garrett, you look great.

GARRETT: You're just saying that because you don't like fuss. Well, brace yourself, because I'm about to make one. No! You're not putting that dorky tie on me! Where's my baseball jacket? Where's my...?

Garrett screeched as Amy sat with him in the suite's living room and tried to snap on the little blue-and-white polka-dot tie that matched the cummerbund on his one-piece white shirt and blue pants. The placket of the shirt was decorated with colorfully embroidered zoo animals.

The girls' outfits matched, except that they had flared skirts rather than pants.

Amy longed for Tom's helping hand, but he'd watched the babies while she showered, so he was still dressing.

"Can I help?" Beau appeared in an elegant blue-and-white pin-striped suit and a subdued tie. He gave Amy a cautious smile. "I got pretty good with him yesterday while Tom was out."

Amy recovered quickly from surprise. "Ah...yes. Please. He's just like his father. Hates to get dressed up."

That was true, she thought defensively. Nate hated formal occasions.

Garrett went to Beau's lap without complaint, but continued to resist when Amy tried to snap on the bow.

"A formal occasion calls for a tie, Garrett," Beau said reasonably, capturing the little hands that tried to interfere with Amy. "There are some rules you just can't get around. Although, I'm with you. A standard tie is so much less dandy."

Amy laughed with him at his joke, and that made Garrett laugh. While he was distracted, Amy snapped on the bow.

Before she could congratulate herself on her success, Peggy marched through in full wedding regalia, complete with veiled pillbox headpiece.

The dress had been lovingly tailored to her every curve, and her long, slender legs made the handkerchief hemline sway as she went past. But Amy noticed that though the bridal dress and veil looked beautiful, the bride did not. She was pale and wounded-looking as she headed determinedly for the door.

"Peggy?" Jane, also dressed for the wedding in the gown that matched Amy's, came hurrying out of her bedroom. She had Malia in her arms. Chelsea had wandered in to visit Sabina and Nelson. "Do you want to borrow my pearl earrings? Peggy?"

Peggy opened the door and kept going as though she hadn't seen or heard anyone.

Amy caught Jane's eye and read the same concern she felt.

"Could you keep an eye on Garrett for a minute?" she asked Beau.

"Sure."

"And her, too?" Jane asked, and deposited Malia on his other knee without waiting for an answer.

Amy ran after Peggy and Jane followed.

Peggy stood in front of a door at the far end of the corridor. She was knocking incessantly on the door, demanding admission.

"Peggy, what...?" Amy began.

The door was yanked open before she could finish, and Ethan stood there in pajama bottoms, chest bare, hair tousled, and a look of blatant insolence on his face.

A young woman wrapped in a towel was visible behind him in the middle of the room.

Peggy was breathing heavily and her face was crumpling. "You promised me this wouldn't happen again," she said.

He put a hand to her arm. "Honey, I didn't..."

"I call you the morning of our wedding," she interrupted, "to tell you I love you, and a *woman* answers?"

Ethan sighed, as though the burden of explanation

was beneath him. "She spent the night with Bill," he said. "You just jumped to conclusions."

Bill Channing also appeared behind Ethan, and Amy saw a look of surprised uncertainty cross Peggy's face.

Amy didn't believe him for a minute.

"I'd like to come inside," Peggy said firmly.

Ethan studied her with disdain. "That would be a violation of my privacy."

Peggy walked around him into the room. Amy and Jane followed.

"You're a *star*, Ethan," Peggy said, underlining the word with scorn. "You don't have any privacy." She found a closed door and threw it open. Another young woman with bright red hair lay in a large bed with the covers pulled up to her chin. There were enough clothes strewn around to suggest there'd been an animated foursome in the bed.

Peggy slammed the door closed and turned to face Ethan. The girl in the towel ran out the door.

Channing sat down at a table by the window, his face in his hands.

Ethan went to the coffeepot behind the bar and calmly poured a cup. "I warned you that I had difficulty being faithful," he said, striding back around the bar.

Peggy yanked off her veil. "Later, you said I'd made you change your mind. That you'd love me always."

He shrugged. "And I will. Only not exclusively."

Peggy flew at him, screaming, hitting, kicking. He screamed as hot coffee splashed on his chest.

Channing rose from the table to pull at Peggy as Amy ran to try to pull the combatants apart. Ethan tried to push her aside and she pushed back.

She never was sure what happened next except that she was yanked away and the small fracas seemed to turn into a riot. Fists flew, men shouted and grunted, and every time she tried to look up from the sofa on which she'd been thrown to see what was happening, lights flashed, blinding her. She wondered idly if she'd sustained a concussion without noticing that she'd been hit. But that made no sense.

When order was finally established, Ethan and Channing were on the floor, out cold, and Tom and Beau stood over them, bruised and mussed, their suits in disarray.

Ethan's mother was in a chair, and Sabina fanned her with the room service menu.

Ethan's father knelt over his son. He glanced up, eyes dark and angry. "Which one of you hit him?" he asked of Tom and Beau.

"I did," Tom replied.

The man glanced toward the room where the young woman in the bed was clearly visible and now crying hysterically. He stood and extended his hand.

"My thanks," he said. "If you discounted my son's good looks, he'd be worthless. Unfortunately, he's able to make money on them. You should have broken his nose. That might have changed things."

"My intention wasn't to break anything," Tom replied quietly. "He pushed at my wife and I just jumped into the middle. My...brother-in-law came to help."

Amy heard his explanation with a crackling flare of excitement. It was adrenaline, she told herself.

Ethan's father shook Beau's hand, as well. "Bill Channing's the same caliber. I'll square things with hotel security. Come along, Dora." He took his wife's arm and pulled her from the sofa. She looked as though she might collapse at any moment.

Sabina was beside herself. "I see no reason why we should be hasty here," she said, now fanning herself with the menu as she got to her feet. "Perhaps Ethan has an explanation for..."

"He does have an explanation, Mother," Peggy said. "They were four in a bed!"

"But the..." Sabina pointed down, in the direction of the garden room where the wedding was scheduled to take place in a matter of minutes.

"The wedding's off, Mom," Peggy insisted. "Face it. I apologize for embarrassing you, Mr. and Mrs. Brennan, but I can't..."

Julian Brennan took her in his arms for a moment. "Of course you can't. Don't worry about us. Ethan's embarrassed us quite a few times in his life. I'll also explain to the hotel caterer. Most of the guests who aren't family were friends of ours, anyway. You don't even have to make an appearance downstairs if you don't want to." He smiled apologetically at the rest of the family. "I'm sorry. I thought success might have taught him some humility. It does that for some people. But apparently not. I'm sure this is best all around. We enjoyed meeting you. I'm sure your beautiful daughter will find a man worthy of her."

"Thank you." Sabina walked the Brennans to the door.

"But...Ethan." Dora pointed to her son, just beginning to stir on the carpet.

"I'm a doctor, darling. He's fine." Julian guided her firmly out the door.

Jane ushered everyone back to the bridal suite.

Amy caught Tom's arm. "Thank you for coming to our rescue," she whispered, smiling. "Technically, I guess women aren't supposed to want protectors anymore, but you dispensed with him more efficiently than I was doing."

He inclined his head modestly. "I had a little lapse into d'Artagnan. It was my pleasure."

Amy gasped suddenly. "The babies!" she cried, and ran on ahead, horrified that she hadn't given the triplets—God, now *she* was doing it!—the babies a thought since she'd left Garrett with Beau. But Beau was now behind her. Had her father been left with all three babies?

When Amy reached the suite, he was almost blithering, and all three babies were screaming.

GARRETT: Not only do you dress me up like some cutesy ad for toilet tissue, but then you *leave* me!

MALIA: He never even turned on the television!

CHELSEA: Did we miss the wedding? Did you bring me any cake?

Amy went straight to the refrigerator, knowing food would quell the noise. Tom picked up Malia, Peggy lifted Chelsea, unmindful of little shoes on the skirt of her wedding dress, and Jane watched in fascination as Beau scooped Garrett into his arms.

The screams of rage quieted to simple anger and, at the sight of string cheese, stopped altogether. Everyone converged on the sofas, babies distributed among them and eating greedily.

Amy watched her mother cry into a floral hanky, and accepted with a new lease on reality that she was crying as much for the contacts she'd lost as for Peggy's unhappiness.

Her father was patting her mother's shoulder and telling her not to worry, that everything would be all right.

Her mother ignored him and wept on.

Jane kicked her shoes off and propped her feet on

the coffee table with a distinct lack of the decorum that usually defined her. "Did I hear you tell that bum that he'd promised you 'it wouldn't happen *again?*'" she demanded of Peggy.

Peggy nodded.

"You mean he'd cheated on you already and you were still going to marry him?"

Peggy's response was to stare at her hands.

"Why?" Amy asked. "You're a beautiful model with the potential for a film career, and he's a classless idiot who treated you badly."

"But *People* magazine voted him..." Sabina began tearfully.

Jane turned to her with a murderous look and she subsided.

"I don't know." Peggy curled into her corner of the sofa and Amy thought she didn't look like a star at all. She looked frightened and alone. "Hollywood's different, you know? Being a celebrity you get caught up in the scene. And make-believe and reality get all twisted around. I guess I thought he was Joey Karminski, the Cleveland cop who was hard as nails but treated his girlfriend like a queen. And I was lonely. I mean, there are always a lot of people around me, but most of them care about how big the next offer is, not about me, particularly."

"Then, don't stay there," Amy said. "If you're not happy, you don't have to be there."

"But...she's about to become a star!" Sabina protested, the hanky pressed to her mouth.

"Why don't you come home with us?" Jane suggested. "If you don't like Boston, you can visit Amy and Tom and check out Heron Point."

Peggy looked from one sister to the other in amazement. "You know...I've lived my whole life thinking that you guys hated me because I was the youngest. I had no idea you even cared, much less that you'd come to my defense with Ethan." She focused on Tom and on Beau. "And the two of you. Thank you. I hope Denny Brewer doesn't ruin your lives."

"Denny Brewer?" Tom asked.

"The photographer for *Star Snaps*. He must have gotten wind of the wedding, somehow. I saw him in the doorway of Ethan's suite, shooting like crazy."

Tom turned to Amy. She read the message in his eyes very clearly. "We're dead."

Peggy drew a deep breath and smiled. It looked less Hollywood, Amy thought, and more genuine. "I think I might have married him, anyway," Peggy said, patting Amy's hand, "if I hadn't seen what a great life you and Tom have. I think it clarified my confusion over make-believe and reality. Tom's always there to help you with the babies, he always speaks to you with respect, and when he touches you—" she rubbed her arms as though to erase a bad memory "—it seems to be always tenderly. I want passion, of course, but I want to be treated like a woman, not a…an appliance."

Jane caught Amy's eye. Amy knew she was remembering their discussion in the dressing room. Then she turned to Beau seated beside her, still holding Garrett, and her face softened. She moved in closer. Apparently pleased, he looped an arm around her.

Her parents sat arm in arm on the love seat, obviously confused and upset.

Amy studied everyone else in the room before she finally turned to Tom. The guilt she'd been warding off since she'd first introduced Tom as her husband back in Heron Point now fell on her like a ton of bricks.

She had to believe her deception had brought about

a good thing, but did the end justify the means in this case?

Tom's dark eyes met hers steadily and told her without words that he thought it was time to come clean.

"You're absolutely right," Amy said, taking Peggy's hand. "You deserve to be appreciated and treated well. But I have to tell you…something."

Peggy patted her hand and turned toward her, waiting. "What is it?"

Amy sensed everyone else's attention turn in her direction. She felt a new and very real fear.

This trip had taught her that she did love her parents, but as sensible and responsible human beings they were—as she'd always suspected—pretty hopeless.

But at the same time, she'd found something new in her relationships with her sisters. They hadn't learned to work together as children and to support and defend one another—but they seemed to be doing it now. Maybe blood was thicker than whatever tried to stand against it. She and Jane had closed ranks when they thought Peggy needed help.

It was curious, Amy thought in a still reasonable corner of her mind, that at the moment when she appeared to have the upper hand over her sisters—a moment she'd dreamed about since she was eight or nine—she was not only not going to lord it over them, she was about to admit to being the worst of them all.

"Tom and I aren't married," she said in a breathless rush.

Everyone stared at her, and there was a moment of absolute silence. Jane turned to Beau, then both turned to Amy and Tom in dual astonishment.

Sabina gasped, and Nelson, still not recovered from having been left with the babies, looked as though he was about to dissolve into a puddle of stress.

Peggy put her free hand to her mouth.

Amy felt curiously cut off from everyone—even Tom, because she could no longer pretend, even to herself, that they were in love.

Then she felt his hand on her shoulder. It squeezed gently. The action gave her courage.

She went on to try to explain how she'd always felt inadequate and outside of the family unit. "It was never that I didn't love you," she explained hastily. "But that I always felt like a misfit. A disappointment." She smiled at Jane. "You were always so beautiful and so smart." She squeezed Peggy's hand. "And you were such a personality from the very beginning. I always felt like a mistake."

Her parents were studying each other in puzzlement. Amy knew they would never understand, but she wanted her sisters to know how she felt. "Tom…" She laced her fingers in the hand he'd placed on her shoulder. "Tom is a carpenter who is renovating a barn on my property, and he'd come in yesterday morning to help me with a plumbing problem. When you all arrived without warning, I wanted you to think I was as happy and successful as you all were because I thought this was going to be one of your every-other-year, two-hour visits." She smiled at Tom. "Tom went along with it because he's a good friend, and I'm sure he didn't want to embarrass me in front of you. When you invited us to come to Seattle, and we went into the bedroom to talk about it, he didn't want to lie to you, but I insisted."

Her sisters still appeared speechless, but Beau asked logically, "But the triplets…"

Amy laughed lightly, thinking that she was going to have some explaining to do when she got home.

"They're the babies of some friends of ours who are away for the weekend. I'm just baby-sitting for them."

"But they love you and Tom," Sabina said.

Amy nodded. "They come to my day care a couple of times a week, and Malia is really Tom's niece, and the other two babies belong to his good friends, so they're used to him."

"I have to lie down," Sabina said. "Nelson, darling, will you help me?"

It was just like her, Amy thought, to miss the real issue. She'd understood nothing Amy had tried to explain.

"Of course, dear. Now, don't worry about a thing." He took her arm and started to walk her to their room. "Everything will be all right."

Amy studied Peggy. "You did the right thing in telling Ethan to take a hike, even though my marriage isn't real. I don't think you did it because of me, I think you did it because you know you're smart and talented and gorgeous, and that settling for anything less than love and fidelity from a man would be stupid."

Peggy twisted her lips in wry denial. "I think I did it because I knew I had backup. You and Janie were right behind me, looking like a matched pair of avenging angels. It gave me courage."

Jane came to sit on an edge of the coffee table facing Amy and Peggy. "Good. And we're going to continue to do that for you, even if we have to do it from opposite ends of the country. And you..." She turned her determined blue eyes on Amy. "You were just reacting to the same insecurities Peggy and I have, so stop looking so guilty. If you hadn't come here with us..." She frowned and shook her head, her manner grave. "I knew I had relatives, but I didn't really understand that I had sisters until we all got together for this wedding."

She leaned forward to wrap them in her embrace. "And this is what's important. We have one another."

Peggy looked a little anxiously in the direction of their parents' bedroom. "I feel badly that Mom's so disappointed."

Jane shook her. "Stop it. She doesn't get it. She never did, she never will. That's not our fault. And Dad sort of gets it, but he doesn't want to have to deal with any difficulties, so he pretends they don't exist." She hugged Amy again. "If you hadn't been there for me to talk to in the dressing room yesterday afternoon, I might have imploded. Thank you for that."

"You're welcome," Amy replied. "Thank you for forgiving me for the lie."

Jane shook her head, denying that it had a negative effect. "If it hadn't been for seeing you so happy—or thinking you were—I wouldn't have talked to Beau like you suggested and straightened everything out." She smiled in his direction. Beau was now chasing all the babies around the other sofa. The babies were giggling hysterically.

She turned back to her sisters. "And if Peggy hadn't seen you and Tom and realized life had something more to offer than Ethan was willing to give her, she might have married the bum. So, see? It all worked out for the best."

Jane leaned around Amy to smile at Tom—only to discover that he was no longer there. The sound of water running turned all heads in the direction of the kitchen. Tom was making a fresh pot of coffee, apparently deciding to leave the women to their rediscovery of one another.

Jane frowned at his broad back, then at Amy. "We've agreed that it doesn't matter that you tricked us, but if you're trying to trick yourself into believing you shouldn't be married to Tom Nicholas, you're making a big mistake.''

"You seem so comfortable together," Peggy said quietly.

"We were involved once," Amy admitted. "But that's over."

"Is it?" Jane asked pointedly.

Amy rolled her eyes. "Please don't worry about me. I'll be fine."

Jane shook her head at her. "And who does *that* sound like?"

AMY WANTED TO EXPLAIN to Tom that she was getting a new perspective on her life, that her priorities had shifted over the past few days, and she was beginning to realize that she didn't have as much to prove as she thought she did. At least, not to her family.

But there was no time. Peggy had to be at the airport at four, and they had to leave for Heron Point that night so that Amy would be at the day care in the morning.

The babies kept them busy during the brief flight, then she'd said goodbye to her parents. Her mother had recovered somewhat, though Amy guessed it would be some time before she was herself again.

"I don't know where you get this about your being a disappointment," Sabina said, pulling Amy aside at the little Heron Point airport. "That's never been true. We just wanted you to be happy, that's all. And…usually we're happier when we *do* things, *have* things." Then she'd kissed her cheek and said, "Dear Amy." There was a little pity in the sound, but at least she hadn't called her "poor Amy."

Her father told her not to worry about a thing, that her mother would get over "the disappointment."

Amy congratulated herself on being mature enough

to accept that she loved her parents and always would. She simply couldn't feel the respect for them that gave the child-parent bond the depth and texture Jave and Tom had for their mother, or Jo Jeffries for her dad. But she decided that was all right. She would take what she could get.

But when she hugged Jane goodbye, she felt the strength of new friendship there. And Beau hugged her with a new vitality and a subtle smile. It pleased Amy that she'd helped bring about a renewal of their love. She'd overheard them talking on the flight and Jane now knew that Beau had been working long hours to buy the house she'd admired and that he thought would make her happy. She'd told him that having his baby would make her happy, and he'd promised to do his utmost to see that she was pregnant by Christmas.

Amy wished she could make her own future look as good as Jane's did at that moment.

She was determined to talk to Tom when they got back to the house, but the babies were fussy and Tom's pager beeped.

He returned the call from Amy's and discovered it was his mother calling from the airport. She'd gotten homesick and caught a last-minute flight home from Europe a week early and wondered if he could pick her up since she couldn't reach Jave.

"Sure, Mom," he said, holding one ear closed against the babies crying behind him. "But it'll take me a couple of hours to get there, so why don't you take the shuttle to the Howard Johnson's, book a room and get some rest if you can until I get there."

"Do I hear babies crying?" she asked hopefully. "Did you come home from Arizona with babies?"

He ran a hand over his face, not minding the two-hour drive to Portland to pick her up, but dreading the two-hour drive back under her interrogation.

"No, Mom," he replied. "I'm working at Amy's day care."

"But it's eleven o'clock on a Sunday night."

He closed his eyes. "It's a long story. I'll explain on the way home."

"Good." She imbued the simple word with great significance. "I'm anxious to see you, Tommy. I love you."

"I love you, too, Mom."

Amy heard the tenderness with which he spoke the words and felt a knot of anguish tighten inside her.

He'd never talked to *her* with that sweet indulgence. Of course, who could blame him?

And she agonized over the realization that he had to leave before she could tell him how she felt. It wasn't something she could blurt out just before he left to drive most of the trip on a dark and winding road.

"Mom's back," he said, hanging up the phone. "I'm going to go pick her up." He looked tired, she thought.

That was no surprise. The weekend had been difficult at best, and because she'd had him turning in a performance most of the time, and doing physical battle in her defense the rest of the time, it had to have been worse than that for him.

"I'll make you a thermos of coffee," she said, turning away to the kitchen.

He caught her arm. "No. I'm wide-awake. You going to be okay with the kids?"

"Sure." Words came to the tip of her tongue. Love words, questions, promises, pleas. But she couldn't turn any of them into sound.

He didn't really look at the moment as though he'd be glad to hear them. Perhaps tomorrow they could talk.

He squeezed her arm gently and left with a simple goodbye.

She wondered for hours afterward if that was what it had been. A simple goodbye.

TOM DROVE THROUGH the black night wondering if arriving home had changed everything. In Seattle she'd needed him, depended upon him, had been relieved to be rescued by him.

But they were back in Heron Point and the fantasy was over. No pretend marriage, no babies that belonged to somebody else. No need for d'Artagnan.

He'd seen a lot of things in her eyes that might have been his imagination—probably were because she hadn't given voice to them.

But then he hadn't realized until he'd met her parents how she must have felt when he'd left two years ago. All she seemed to get from them was artfully subtle rejection. She must have thought that was what she was getting from him.

Well. He was going to have to make it clear to her tomorrow how things were, then he guessed it was pretty much up to her.

It was a good thing he'd be driving home with his mother since he wouldn't be sleeping, anyway.

Chapter Thirteen

Amy noticed Monday morning that Heron Point had a new quality. Part of the difference was seasonal. The rains had come with a vengeance, and Kate reported when she arrived at work after stopping for doughnuts that there were honeycomb paper turkeys in all the shop windows downtown.

The children who came to Kids & Co. on the school bus brought turkeys they'd created at school, and one of the mothers brought a large Pilgrim puzzle. The children watched an afternoon special about the *Mayflower*.

But another part of the difference was that she used to be miserable at Thanksgiving, knowing that almost everyone else but she would be spending it with a loving family.

This year things were different. She wouldn't be able to spend the holiday with her sisters, but she knew they were out there, thinking about her, caring about her.

While she appreciated that, she couldn't help but wonder if that was all she would have. Tom had reported to work this morning without the greeting beep of his horn as he turned up the drive, and he hadn't made one single visit for a cup of coffee.

And she'd been too busy to go to him.

But on the good side—she was able to report to Rodney's father that he was going home without owing the cuss box a penny for that afternoon.

Boomer beamed.

Darcy and Truman, Amy noticed, seemed to have made a curious forward leap in their relationship. Rodney teased her about the Blue Grass Brenda, which was now also out of the box and looking mussy and loved, and Truman told him to stop it.

Rodney had been shocked.

"Just leave her alone," Truman said.

Amy didn't understand until Ginger Billings and Steve Fuller arrived together to pick up their children, and Amy saw that the Friday night pizza they'd been about to share before her own weekend became a three-act play must have developed into something else.

There was a glow in their eyes and the suggestion that Truman already had things figured out and was looking out for his "sister."

The six parents of Amy's "triplets" returned as planned about seven Monday evening to pick up their children. They brought Aggie Nicholas, Tom and Jave's mother, with them. Tom was working late on the barn.

Jave sat on the sofa with an excited Malia in his arms, and Nancy sat beside him, Pete pressing in between them and Eddy leaning in on her other side, showing her leaves he'd collected on the Boy Scout trip. Aggie, a plump, gray-haired woman in green sweats, had taken the room's only rocking chair and smiled at them from across the room. Amy remembered what a rocky beginning the couple had had and found herself smiling over the warm unit they'd become.

Chelsea climbed into the chair where Jo sat, Ryan sitting on the arm, and told her parents a long story that made no sense, but seemed to include a "plane." They, too, had struggled to find common ground when Ryan's wife, Jo's sister, had died. But they'd found it in Chelsea in the most rewarding way.

Nate and Karma sat cross-legged on the floor as Garrett showed them the book about turkeys one of the other mothers had brought. For a romance that had begun in the ER at Riverview Hospital, it looked very healthy to Amy.

Amy braced herself as Chelsea continued to talk about a plane. She was going to have to tell these people that she'd taken their children to Seattle. But she and Tom had agreed that no one had to know they'd pretended to be married and passed the children off as theirs.

She prayed she wouldn't lose them as clients. Though she'd agreed to baby-sit as a friend, and not as their day-care provider, absconding with their children with or without her professional hat on was not a commendable thing.

"Ah. I have something to tell you," she said.

She became immediately suspicious when all eyes met across the room, then turned to her.

They knew.

"That's good," Nate said with a smile that did not appear hostile, "because we'd like to talk to you, too."

Jave pulled out a cellular phone and stabbed out a number. "Tom," he said after a moment. "Yeah, we're here at Amy's. I saw the lights on in the barn and figured you were still there. Come to the house. We want to talk to you." He listened a moment. "Well, I don't know," he said. "*Is* everything fine?" He listened again. "Thanks, but you don't have to worry about picking up something for Mom for dinner because Nancy and I picked her up on our way into town and brought her with us. Come and join us." He closed and pocketed the phone. "He'll be right here," he told the group.

"You know that we took your children to Seattle," Amy said, pretty certain the matter was no longer in question. This had all the makings of a confrontation.

"Yes," Ryan replied, "but let's wait for Tom. What do you say we call for pizza?"

There was an immediate discussion about number and toppings, then Nancy, Jo and Karma took over Amy's kitchen, setting the table with paper plates and making coffee.

Tom had taken a few minutes to clean up in the bathroom he'd added in the barn, and appeared at the back door looking startlingly handsome and just a little aggressive.

"My mother's here?" he asked under his breath as Amy let him in.

Amy nodded in concern.

"They're upset about our taking the kids?"

"I think so," she replied, "because I didn't get a chance to tell them. They seem to already know."

"How?"

"No idea. They wanted to wait for you before we discussed it."

He ran a hand over his face. "You and your easy two hours."

"I'm sorry."

"I hope so."

Everyone took a place at the table, except Pete and Eddy, who were allowed to watch television until the pizza arrived, and the babies, who were tricycling around the coffee table in the living room.

Tom went to hug his mother, then took the chair at the head table and remained standing, hands lightly on his hips as he greeted everyone. "Okay," he said. "It was a stupid thing for us to do and we apologize. Amy's back was to the wall with her family and she took her best shot. The kids had a great time, and they were never in any danger or even discomfort. Amy had her cell phone, so if you'd called, you'd have reached her. She did try to call you before we left to make sure you didn't mind our taking the kids, but you guys were in a workshop, and we thought paging you out would only panic you unnecessarily.''

"Wait." Amy, seated at his right, stood and put a staying hand on his arm. "Tom was never in agreement. He objected from the beginning and resisted all along the way, but I had already made retreat impossible and so…he did the gentlemanly thing and came along.''

Jave leaned back in his chair. "Gentlemanly? Really? Nate, check his vital signs.''

Nate shook his head. "Don't have to. He's nuts. I can tell by looking at him.''

Tom gave his brother, then his friend, a lethal glance. "Look. I laid out a couple of pretty big guys this weekend. Don't mess with me.''

"Actually…'' Jo unfolded a newspaper and placed it in the center of the table. "That's what we want to talk about. Although all this other stuff you've alluded to sounds pretty interesting, too. But this, first.'' She tapped her index finger on the front page of the paper. "What in the hell happened?''

Tom and Amy leaned over the table to study the front page of the *Star Snaps* tabloid. In a half-page photo in brilliant color, Tom held Amy with one arm and had just delivered a right cross to Ethan Brennan's face with his fist. Amy, in bridesmaid attire, looked shocked and had obviously just been taken from the other man's grasp. His hand was still curled around her arm, though his head was snapped back and his hair flew out behind him. His large, muscular chest was exposed and naked as he looked about to fall backward.

Beside him, Beau, with perfect boxing club form, had a fist in the stomach of Bill Channing, who was doubled over. Behind him, Jane, dressed just like Amy, had both hands over her face, her wide eyes filled with an avid excitement over the tips of her fingers.

Under the photo, the caption read, *People* Magazine's Second Sexiest Man Felled by World's Smoothest Right Cross. The photo credit belonged to the man Peggy had warned them about—Denny Brewer.

"Tell us," Nancy said, "that this was some scene in an operetta. I mean, you do all look like you were dressed for it. And where were our children at this time?"

Tom sat down with a groan.

Amy sat primly on the edge of her chair, determined to extricate him from the mess.

Carefully, painstakingly, she told the whole story— how she'd always felt like a misfit in her family, how the opportunity to show them a husband and family when they arrived unexpectedly was more of a temptation than she could withstand, and how what she'd expected to be an innocent few hours turned into the weekend from purgatory.

She explained about Ethan Brennan's boorish behavior and Peggy's eleventh-hour march to his room that had yielded a bedmate—three, in fact.

"Oh, my," Aggie said.

"But your babies were safe with my father the whole time," Amy assured everyone. "Honestly. In fact, when my family discovered Tom and I weren't married, their biggest disappointment was that the babies weren't in the family. They even have wedding outfits now if you ever end up going to one."

"So you didn't get married while we were gone?" Jave asked. "This story—" he pointed to the paper "—says you're husband and wife."

Amy shook her head. "No, we're not married."

Aggie closed her eyes in a gesture of relief. "Well, that's good, because I'd have pummeled both of you if you'd gotten married without letting me plan everything."

Nancy smiled blandly at them. "We all want to help. What about a Christmas wedding?"

Amy blinked. "You're not upset that we took the babies to Seattle?"

The three couples looked at one another, then shook their heads.

"It would have been nice if you'd told us," Nancy said, "but we'd trust either of you with them at any time."

Karma grimaced. "But how was it dealing with triplets?"

Amy looked at them in disbelief. Was this all going to end peacefully, after all?

"It was great," Tom said before she could reply. "And do your thing with the Christmas wedding, Mom. As of this weekend, Amy and I are formally engaged."

Aggie and the women shrieked, the men cheered. Jave leveled a steady gaze on Tom, which he returned. Then Jave smiled and applauded with the rest. Aggie leaned over to hug her oldest son.

Amy was thunderstruck. She'd known that a peaceful solution had been too much to hope for. She opened her mouth to correct Tom, because while that was what she wanted, they'd barely exchanged a word all day long. Then she remembered the moment when the tables had been turned and she'd wanted *his* cooperation. He'd given it without embarrassing her. But what was he *doing?*

The doorbell rang, announcing the arrival of the pizza, and there was a flurry of activity as Jo got the door. Karma went to pour soft drinks and Nancy distributed pizza.

Amy beckoned Tom. "Could I speak to you for a minute, please?" she asked sweetly.

"Of course." He grinned at his brother and his friends. "She's insatiable. She wants me all the time."

Guffaws trailed him as he followed her out the back door.

"What are you doing?" she demanded.

The night was cold and she folded her arms, shrinking into her big sweater. Inside, she was shuddering with emotions she didn't understand and was sure were unwarranted.

He leaned a shoulder against the back of the house, his expression visible in the light from the kitchen window. She found it difficult to read. It was hard, she thought, to profess love to a man when you couldn't tell what he was thinking.

"You think you're the only one who can lie through her teeth and expect cooperation?" he asked.

"But that was *my* family, and I thought they were only going to be in town for a couple of hours. These are our friends! And your mother and your brother!"

"Yes, I know." Laughter exploded inside the house and Tom turned toward it and smiled. When he looked back at her again, his expression had softened. "That's why we're going to have to keep it up for longer than a couple of hours."

There was an energy emanating from him that Amy didn't entirely understand. His pose was casual, his manner lazy, yet the air around him, between her and him, was alive with something....

"For how...long?" she asked on a whisper.

"Forty years," he replied quietly. "Fifty, if we're lucky." Then, without warning, he straightened away from the house, caught her arm and pulled her with him to the middle of the field, where he stopped under the big November moon.

The night was alive with sounds, and laughter came again from the house. The scent of fall and wood smoke wound around them.

Tom framed her face in his hands and looked down into her eyes, feeling as though he knew her very well without understanding her at all. He wouldn't have thought that possible.

"Are you going to help me?" he asked.

She looked back at him, and he saw her eyes well with tears. He felt a moment's panic, but then she wrapped her arms around his waist and fell against him. Now he was completely confused.

"I can't," she wept.

He experienced the cold, downward rush of dread. Oh, no. No.

Then she drew back to look at him, her lashes wet and spiked, but she was smiling.

"Because if you want me to lie," she said, "then I'd have to go back in there and tell them I *don't* love you."

He absorbed the words and thought he was about to go insane. Saying she *didn't* love him would be a lie?

Desperately needing his world righted, he took her arms and shook her lightly. "Say it directly, Amy!" he demanded.

The night wind circled them, lifting her hair, carrying her jasmine scent to his nostrils. "I love you, Tom," she whispered, then stood on tiptoe and kissed him with all the passion and fervor in her heart.

Amy was crushed in Tom's arms as he returned her kisses. He lifted her off the grass and swung her in a circle. Everything that had ever stood between them disintegrated, and all the feelings and dreams that had lingered on the edges of their lives awaiting a nourishing atmosphere rushed in to tighten their embrace.

"Amy, I love you," he said against her cheek. "I'm going to cherish you so that you'll forget the past and think only about what lies ahead of us."

"I'm sorry I closed the door on you two years ago," she said in a rush. "I was thinking about *me*, not about you and me...."

He silenced her with a kiss. "No, I should have made you understand, but it was easier to be wounded and angry. I was getting really good at that."

"And I want to spend a week on the *Mud Hen.*" She held him tighter, relishing the knowledge that after all this time he was finally hers. "Just give me enough time to warn my clients."

"We'll do it when the barn's finished," he suggested, kissing her hair. "Then you can reopen with a grand opening of the new building."

"Hey!" Jave's voice shouted from the back door. "You'd better come back and defend yourselves. We're planning Thanksgiving, and so far you two are bringing everything!"

Tom waved at Jave. "Be right there."

Amy started toward the house, but Tom pulled her back. He reached into the pocket of his shirt and slipped a marquis-cut diamond on the third finger of her left hand. Then he kissed it.

Amy stared at it, then held it up. Moonlight winked

in it and illuminated a broad band filigreed in heart shapes.

She wrapped her arms around him, speechless with love and joy.

He held her close, his heart too full for words.

The back door opened again, and Jave shouted. "Step on it! Now you're hosting Christmas!"

Epilogue

BABY #1: What's all the noise?

BABY #2: They're singing Christmas carols. Nice, isn't it? Did you hear all those people and kids? We must have a big family and lots of friends.

BABY #1: Yeah. Lucky. I can't wait for her to tell him we're here. Then we'll get some of the attention all those bigger babies are getting.

BABY #2: She said she was going to tell him tonight— that we're going to be a Christmas present. But even she doesn't know there are two of us yet.

BABY #1: I bet they'd have liked us better if you were a boy, too.

BABY #2: No way. One boy and one girl is supposed to make a perfect family.

BABY #1: They sound pretty perfect. I like the way she laughs, and I like the sound of his voice.

BABY #2: I like it when he holds us all tight. Yep. There he is. Can you feel his arms around us?

BABY #1: Mmm. Yeah.

BABY #2: I think we got really lucky. Merry Christmas.

BABY #1: Yeah, Merry Christmas. Whoa. Somebody out there's off-key.

BABY #2: Sounds beautiful to me.

EVER HAD ONE OF THOSE DAYS?

TO DO:

☑ late for a super-important meeting, you discover the cat has eaten your panty hose

☑ while you work through lunch, the rest of the gang goes out and finds a one-hour, once-in-a-lifetime 90% off sale at the most exclusive store in town (Oh, and they also get to meet Brad Pitt who's filming a movie across the street.)

☑ you discover that your intimate phone call with your boyfriend was on company-wide intercom

☑ finally at the end of a long and exasperating day, you escape from it all with an entertaining, humorous and always romantic Love & Laughter book!

ENJOY
LOVE & LAUGHTER™
EVERY DAY!

For a preview, turn the page....

Here's a sneak peek at
Colleen Collins's RIGHT CHEST, WRONG NAME
Available August 1997...

―――――――――

"DARLING, YOU SOUND like a broken cappuccino machine," murmured Charlotte, her voice oozing disapproval.

Russell juggled the receiver while attempting to sit up in bed, but couldn't. If he *sounded* like a wreck over the phone, he could only imagine what he looked like.

"What mischief did you and your friends get into at your bachelor's party last night?" she continued.

She always had a way of saying "your friends" as though they were a pack of degenerate water buffalo. Professors deserved to be several notches higher up on the food chain, he thought. Which he would have said if his tongue wasn't swollen to twice its size.

"You didn't do anything...bad...did you, Russell?"

"Bad." His laugh came out like a bark.

"Bad as in *naughty*."

He heard her piqued tone but knew she'd never admit to such a base emotion as jealousy. Charlotte Maday, the woman he was to wed in a week, came from a family who bled blue. Exhibiting raw emotion was akin to burping in public.

After agreeing to be at her parents' pool party by

noon, he untangled himself from the bed sheets and stumbled to the bathroom.

"Pool party," he reminded himself. He'd put on his best front and accommodate Char's request. Make the family rounds, exchange a few pleasantries, play the role she liked best: the erudite, cultured English literature professor. After fulfilling his duties, he'd slink into some lawn chair, preferably one in the shade, and nurse his hangover.

He tossed back a few aspirin and splashed cold water on his face. Grappling for a towel, he squinted into the mirror.

Then he jerked upright and stared at his reflection, blinking back drops of water. "Good Lord. They stuck me in a wind tunnel."

His hair, usually neatly parted and combed, sprang from his head as though he'd been struck by lightning. "Can too many Wild Turkeys do that?" he asked himself as he stared with horror at his reflection.

Something caught his eye in the mirror. Russell's gaze dropped.

"What in the—"

Over his pectoral muscle was a small patch of white. A bandage. Gingerly, he pulled it off.

Underneath, on his skin, was not a wound but a small, neat drawing.

"A red heart?" His voice cracked on the word *heart*. Something—a word?—was scrawled across it.

"Good Lord," he croaked. "I got a tattoo. A heart tattoo with the name Liz on it."

Not Charlotte. Liz!

**HARLEQUIN AND SILHOUETTE
ARE PLEASED TO PRESENT**

Love, marriage—and the pursuit of family!

Check your retail shelves for these upcoming titles:

July 1997
Last Chance Cafe by Curtiss Ann Matlock
The most determined bachelor in Oklahoma is in trouble! A
lovely widow with three daughters has moved next door—and
the girls want a dad! But he wants to know if their mom needs
a husband....

August 1997
Thorne's Wife by Joan Hohl
Pennsylvania. It was only to be a marriage of convenience—
until they fell in love! Now, three years later, tragedy
threatens to separate them forever and Valerie wants only to
be in the strength of her husband's arms. For she has some
very special news for the expectant father...

September 1997
Desperate Measures by Paula Detmer Riggs
New Mexico judge Amanda Wainwright's daughter has been
kidnapped, and the price of her freedom is a verdict in
favor of a notorious crime boss. So enters ex-FBI agent
Devlin Buchanan—ruthless, unstoppable—and soon there is
no risk he will not take for her.

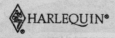 

HARLEQUIN WOMEN KNOW ROMANCE WHEN THEY SEE IT.

And they'll see it on **ROMANCE CLASSICS**, the new 24-hour TV channel devoted to romantic movies and original programs like the special **Harlequin** Showcase of Authors & Stories.

The **Harlequin** Showcase of Authors & Stories introduces you to many of your favorite romance authors in a program developed exclusively for Harlequin readers.

Watch for the **Harlequin** Showcase of Authors & Stories series beginning in the summer of 1997.

If you're not receiving ROMANCE CLASSICS, call your local cable operator or satellite provider and ask for it today!

Escape to the network of your dreams.

ROMANCE CLASSICS

And the Winner Is...
You!

...when you pick up these great titles
from our new promotion at your
favorite retail outlet this June!

Diana Palmer
The Case of the Mesmerizing Boss

Betty Neels
The Convenient Wife

Annette Broadrick
Irresistible

Emma Darcy
A Wedding to Remember

Rachel Lee
Lost Warriors

Marie Ferrarella
Father Goose

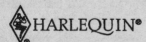 

HARLEQUIN® Silhouette®

Look us up on-line at: http://www.romance.net ATWI397-R

mommy + me

If you loved this newest Mommy and Me tale by

MURIEL JENSEN

Don't miss the three stories that started it all:

Harlequin American Romance®

#16603	MOMMY ON BOARD	$3.50	U.S. ☐
		$3.99	CAN.☐
#16606	MAKE WAY FOR MOMMY	$3.50	U.S. ☐
		$3.99	CAN.☐
#16610	MERRY CHRISTMAS, MOMMY	$3.50	U.S. ☐
		$3.99	CAN.☐

(limited quantities available on certain titles)

TOTAL AMOUNT	$
POSTAGE & HANDLING	$
($1.00 for one book, 50¢ for each additional)	
APPLICABLE TAXES*	$ _____
TOTAL PAYABLE	$ _____

(check or money order—please do not send cash)

To order, complete this form and send it, along with a check or money order for the total above, payable to Harlequin Books, to: **In the U.S.:** 3010 Walden Avenue, P.O. Box 9047, Buffalo, NY 14269-9047; **In Canada:** P.O. Box 613, Fort Erie, Ontario, L2A 5X3.

Name: _____

Address: _____ City: _____

State/Prov.: _____ Zip/Postal Code: _____

*New York residents remit applicable sales taxes.
Canadian residents remit applicable GST and provincial taxes. HMJBACK1

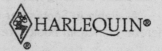
HARLEQUIN®